Novels by Adrienne Nash

The Quartet. 'Trudi'; ~ 'Trudi in Paris';

'Trudi and Simon'; ~ 'Trudi without Simon'.

'Breakdown'.

'Long Journey into Light'.

'Castle Murkie'.

'The Trials of Sienna Chambers'.

'The Cellar'; ~ and sequel, ~ 'A Time to be Brave'.

'Elizabeth'.

'A Strange Life'. (Autobiography of the Author)

'Tina G.'

'To Love and Love Not.'

'Coming Out'.

'From the Ashes' and the se

'Prejudice and Sensitivities'.

'Something Good out of the Bad.'

'Holly.'

'So We Grew Together.'

'Lost in the Snow.'

'Owing Lili.'

'Wide Skies' by Adrienne May and Brian Watts.

'The Passing of Little Tough Guy.'

Please leave a review.

The Passing of Little Tough Guy.

by Adrienne Nash

Chapter 1.

I've been in residential childcare for the last five years, ever since my dad was sent to jail and mum ended up in psychiatric care. See dad was found guilty of armed robbery and GBH with intent, having cracked the skull of a security man when he did the bank job. Dad's a lifer, and the judge set a tariff of ten years, so he still has four years more.

Not that I'm bothered. He can rot in hell. When I was eight, I worshipped my dad. He was always fun with me, though he rowed all the time with mum. I grew up thinking why would anyone ever get married if this is what living with someone meant. I'm afraid I thought mum was just a nag because dad used to get it in the neck as soon as he came through the door. Sometimes she chucked a pot at him, or anything else that came to hand. It was just like those old cartoons where the wife stands behind the door with her rolling pin. She heard his car and she armed up. He seldom retaliated other than to grab her and restrain her in a bear hug. He would present her with some trinket, which sometimes she would stamp on. Then he would act all hurt, that he had thought of her and bought a present and she had destroyed it. That was usually followed by a truce. He'd be good enough for a few days and then he would be off. I didn't know what was going on, just thought he was away working, never knew he was a criminal. I never knew he had a mistress.

That was life for me growing up. I had a brother once. He died when I was three and he was six, so I hardly remember. He ran out after a football and was hit by a car. Dad told me about it, as a lesson to be aware on the street. Gordon my brother was thrown thirty feet by the collision. Kids were driving a stolen car. The moral of this story dad told me, was always look when going into the road and always be aware on the street. He never moralised about stealing the car or about speeding. I never realised then but I do now, my dad was amoral. Oh he could be fun and he would buy a mate a pint but when it came to theft, robbery, beating someone, it was the law of the jungle and my dad, only five feet eight inches, was a lion.

Poor mum, she couldn't believe that her fun loving jovial husband could have done such a thing as robbing a security van. Yeah they rowed but she loved the bastard. She knew he had faults, never keeping a job for more than eighteen months but somehow he managed to keep the money coming in. He'd be out of work, go absent leaving mum scraping the pennies from the vase on the top shelf in the pantry. Then he'd reappear when mum was wringing her hands and waiting to be paid at the end of the week for her office cleaning job, no money and no food in the house. He'd drop notes on the kitchen table and there would be a snarling argument.

If dad was a lion, then mum was too. She could be vicious and if she'd had the jaws and teeth of a lion, she

4

would have seized him by the throat and choked the life out of him. Oh yes, girls can be vicious too and god help men if the female animal possessed as much strength as the male. See that's another thing where the lion analogy is apt. In the wild pride, it is the females who hunt and the man bosses everyone about but when a female's cubs are threatened by a male, he better watch out if he fancies keeping his balls. That's where I think God was wise because a woman of equal strength to man, would be a formidable animal if roused.

Then came the final scene in their marriage. He and two mates did this bank in South London, down Tooting way. The guy from the security van defended not only himself but the box he carried. Dad hit him with a crow bar but the guy clung to the box and the chain cutter dad carried, wouldn't cut though the chain in one snip. Cheap rubbish, dad said it was, bought off Bermondsey Market. That's another lesson Dad taught me, if it's a serious thing get the best, like the gold Rolex he stole.

Anyway back to the robbery, the alarm was ringing, dad's mates took off and two police in a passing Panda[1] gave chase but dad escaped with the box. We went on holiday to South West Wales, a tiny cottage on the cliff edge. As soon as we returned, the police nabbed him. Fifteen years of crime had come to an end. He swore vengeance on his brother and his mate.

---

[1] Panda is a local small patrol car named after the black and white colours.

5

Me and mum were left more or less penniless, living on the State and her bit of cleaning money. It was discovered at the trial, he also had a mistress and when he was supposed to be working nights or away on a road-building contract he was living in a caravan with Leanne. He hadn't actually had a proper job for years. We had lived on the profits of his crimes.

That's all why mum had a breakdown.

That's why I went to foster parents, Mr and Mrs Downey. I was horrible. Even though they were experienced handling damaged kids, I was too much. I was in a prolonged sulk. Nothing was right. I was horrible too at school, disruptive. I cried a lot and when I wasn't crying I hit out. I was so disturbed that I couldn't even learn. Like given something to read, a chapter of history even like someone interesting like King John, even if I read it, nothing would stick in my memory. I could read a page and by the end would remember nothing because all this other stuff was going on in my head. It was like with a computer, trying to write something while a massive download is happening and what you want to do just doesn't happen and gets jumbled. My brain was just mush, like a machine full of washing. Looking through the window you try and concentrate on the shirt, but there's pants, bras, and stuff whirling about blurring vision.

So the Downeys and me only last three months. They were good people and I don't blame them. I went into a home and then more fostering when the lady from childcare thought I was ready. The Adler family was large, four of their own and two other foster kids. Joe the boy foster kid hated me from the start and I don't know why, except I liked his sister Jenny. She was so pretty and had this way of looking out the side of her big chestnut eyes. We was Jenny and me, good friends, I mean I was fascinated by her and liked her company more than the boys. Anyway Joe picked and picked at me and told lies and in the end, I did what dad would have told me to do, I hit him solidly in the throat, aiming for his jaw. He went to hospital and I went back to the home. Joe recovered. I had established a record. I was told I was lucky not to go to young offenders. They said I was on the path to end in prison like my dad.

My mum came out of care and then relapsed. I go and see her and she's a zombie, hardly knows I'm there. She's so passive, just no will even to chat. I go and see her but dread it. She's on these pills and stuff that have taken away all her emotions. She's just the walking breathing shell of the once pretty, feisty girl she had been. I hate my dad for I blame him. Fucking bastard.

Here I am. Nearly fifteen and no good. My exam results will be rubbish, I know that even before I done the exams. Then as soon as I'm sixteen, the Council will be preparing me to go into a flat on my own when I'm eighteen, so I'll have two years of transition. The

Government say that those in foster care can now stay there till twenty-one and will be monitored till twenty-five. The future looks pretty black to me. I don't want to be like dad but I'm fucking frightened that's how I'll end up. I don't like myself a lot. See there's other stuff going on in my head and I'm so angry. Angry with the home, angry with what the doctors done to mum, angry with school and some of the kids there and angry with this children's home.

Above all, I'm angry with myself because I'm not the person I want to be. Life is a big disappointment in so many ways and gets worse year by year.

Chapter 2.

Look I've spent half an hour telling you how bad I am, what a loser, and you probably think I should just get myself together, be, and here's a new word I learnt, be pragmatic, like realistic and make the best of what I have. Clear the trash out of my brain, forget the bad hand of cards I've been dealt and just get on with life.

See the trouble is, that there's other things going on in my head, things I can't tell no one, or is that anyone. English is not my best subject, well actually I don't have a best subject, only worst.

Like anyone who makes a suggestion that I'm less of a boy because I dress neat and keep myself clean, then I lash out and as I already told, I may be small but I know how to hurt and where to do the most damage. See I have this temper, I see red and because of the hang-ups my ego is like a balloon and easily pricked.

There's this kid in the home called Amal, I don't know where he's from and nor do I think he knows either, but he started on me as soon as I come to the home, because he was brown and I was white and I looked like neat and tidy and he's a scruff, he's a gangle, sixteen and near six foot tall and me, I'm just five five. So he sees his sort of opposite, especially as he is noisy, boisterous and a thug and a bully and I just want to be left alone.

So I come in from school and I drop my bag and he boots it across the hallway, books spilling out and the cover coming off my notebook. I don't want that cause I have sketches in there that are for my eyes only.

Then the bastard kicks me in the thigh and I have an instant dead leg and fall down and he laughs and moves off. He says, 'Fucking girly boy.'

Now that is something he has said before, because I am compared to him. I mean I'm clean. I wash my hair and I keep my clothes clean and cut my nails and scrub them. I have a mane of blond hair, long, maybe he thinks me a girly and I don't care, just leave me the fuck alone. It's none of his business how I am and I'm not going to be a scruff to please him.

When I get my leg moving, I collect my stuff together and hang my bag from the peg marked Peter Wallace. I go in search of Amal who is now fooling about on the table tennis, just messing someone's game. That's what he does, the Home bully, the one the other kids hate and avoid if possible.

So I walk up behind him and tap him on the shoulder and first he doesn't even turn around, he's having so much fun messing with these kids. So I stick a finger in his arse area and this time he jerks around as though he's been raped. As he turns, I hit him in the throat and he sort of jack knives, like doubles and I knee him in the balls. He falls and the tennis table collapses. The heavy top lands on a hand and his wrist snaps, I swear I heard it or perhaps that was the bat falling on the floor.

Well he is just about out for the count but not quite, but he's hurt enough that he can't retaliate. Mr Robins one of the carers comes in and asks what's going on.

'Sir we wuz playing and Amal took a great swipe at the ball and hit the table and it collapsed on him Mr Robins.' Lisa says, quick as a flash, because we are all fed up with Amal.

'Was that how it was Peter?'

'Sir. Exactly sir. I think he's bad hurt sir. He needs attention.' And me being concerned for a dear friend try and help him up, but he don't want to know. He shakes me off and there's real tears in his eyes. 'He's crying like a baby Sir. I think he needs serious treatment.'

So the staff come and he is taken to hospital and returns three hours later his wrist in plaster and his head down.

After that, he was more quiet and left people alone. See that's where Jesus got it wrong. You can't turn the other cheek with people like Amal, because they will plant a fist on the second cheek too. Sometimes a bully needs a thrashing, that's the only way they learn.

That's how the home was. Some bullies, some really damaged kids that cry a lot, some just sulk, some just don't seem to care. All will end up as under achievers and I'm one, too much going on in my head and thoughts that when I see the counsellor, who we all see from time to time, I can't even say, can't tell. It's too shaming and if it ever got out, well my life wouldn't be worth living.

I thought like, when puberty struck, all that would go away, all my bad and awkward thoughts would disappear. These were thoughts that I would hardly tell Dad, the alpha scumbag male that he was and nor could I tell mum either because she had enough troubles and more. As a really small kid and after my brother died, though his death had nothing to do with how I feel I spoke to no one for two weeks mum said. No I was just growing up, my brain was starting to think and to make choices. I used to do dress up like in mum's cast off that of course looked ludicrous and even dad laughed when I had a dress on that fell like a puddle around me and one of mum's wedding hats. They laughed and I laughed. Then I was told not to and it was OK for little kids but not boys, so I didn't no more.

Then there was shopping with mum and she would go to Marks and buy stuff and I would be there and sort of hiding among the stands of bras and knickers and other stuff and I would secretly feel the lovely fabrics and admire the colours. There was so much variety, all different shapes

I suppose to accommodate ladies with different needs and figures, while men's clothes were just basically the same except for size and boring and in either white or really horrid colours, navy and brown and if they were really daring, bright red pants. All ghastly.

When puberty struck, which for me was late, I mean even now at fifteen, nearly, I haven't got a whisker. All the lads my age were saying dirty stuff about girls like they would like to give her ONE and that girl ONE, and we all know what that meant don't we, as though that was all there was to girls, there to satisfy the needs of male hormones, while I was sort of looking at girls different. Like I would look at their arms and compare to mine, or their knees and some people, boys and girls have sort of sticky out knees and others have smooth. Mine were smooth and that mattered to me. Well I don't think it should, I mean not if I'm a boy. Boys aren't bothered about that. They are not much bothered about hair even. Yeah they don't like losing it, but a boy will get up in the morning and perhaps run fingers through the thatch and that's it. Me, I take care of my hair, I buy good shampoo, even though I haven't much money and I use conditioner and I get really annoyed if anyone poaches it.

It's got worser as I grow older. I find I'm constantly looking at girls in school and when I'm in the Mall and comparing with me. I think I do look girly and I do have nice legs but they are stuck in trousers anyway. What I would

13

really love is to wear a skirt and show off my great legs, wind the waist band up and show more thigh like the girls do at school and they are constantly told off for it but keep doing it. I don't blame them.

Then there's hands. I can't stand hands that look as if the owner had clawed their way through a forest, jagged or broken nails, bitten to the quick nails and dirty. See some girls do bite their nails, but most don't and then even in school, there are touches of pretty polish and manicuring and cleanliness. My nails are nice. I want to grow them but if I did, some bugger would soon cotton on and that would be me, little tough guy, gone forever. That is what protects me, my ability to fight dirty, and win even against a thug like Amal.

I have this longing to not be me, to be a girl, even a really thick girl as long as I'm pretty. For a boy I guess actually I am pretty. Mohammed Ali called himself pretty, because that was a gimmick, something to grab attention but in real life, life on the streets or in the home or school, no boy would ever say that about himself. I don't but I think it. I'm not right.

So there you see, I'm a total waste of space. I look into the future and next year we have exams and then depending on that, we go onto sixth-form college. I know I'm going to fail. What then? End up like Dad a no hoper, a scallywag, crook or I go on a building site in grubby overalls and cement dust or wood shavings and learn a trade. There's nothing wrong with that if that is what one wants to do but I don't. I'd like to work in a bank or something, push a pen and go to work as a dolly bird, heels and lipstick, nail polish, smile sweetly and even get my mini skirted tush patted by the boss.

So now, you know just how bent I am, how much of a failure as a boy I am and all these weird thoughts that run through my head, cause me anxiety and make my male life more and more difficult. I thought this might all go away, but it hasn't and all the time I'm getting older and I know the inevitable will happen. I'll become a man and that really is the last thing I want.

I feel so isolated with this secret me struggling to escape. There's no one to help me, mum's like a zombie and Dad would kill me and I trust no one, not even myself.

So it's no wonder that I see most of the world as an enemy, most people as potential enemies. I feel trapped, like I'm against a wall and facing a road roller and I will get squashed.

I no longer see mum much. Probably you think that dreadful, but in my state, I cannot bear seeing mum like that, like she is, just a shadow of what she was. When I go, she hardly says a word I give her a cuddle and feel so little from her in return. Then when I phone to go, they say don't because mum's not well enough. It's horrible. My life is just a waste and I'm really frightened what the future holds.

Dad I never see and hope never to see him again. He did me no physical harm, but he is violent and he has ruined mum's life and maybe mine too.

Chapter 3.

I'm walking down Croydon Mall, the Whitgift Centre. Yeah it's a funny name because when you get there, there are no gifts. There's also a Whitgift Foundation and a Whitgift school and they all get their name from John Whitgift who was an archbishop at the time of Queen Elizabeth the first. That I did learn at school. He must have been a clever guy because those were turbulent times and Good Queen Bess cut off the heads, not personally you understand, of fifty people who displeased her. She was better than her sister Mary who had preceded her, for she cut off more than Lizzie but in a tenth the time.

Why do I know this? 'Blackadder' the TV period comedy. I like to think that Good Queen Bess was like Lizzie in Blackadder rather than the Queen of Hearts in Alice in Wonderland who kept screaming 'off with their heads.' Lizzie in Blackadder is what I learned the other day, mercurial, amoral and capricious, at one moment all over Edmund Blackadder and the next saying he would look rather silly with his head on a pole. Queen Mary on the other hand was a religious bigot decapitating and burning at the stake for religious belief. Six hundred years later that still happens in the Middle East because of religion. One thing I learned from dad, religion ain't no good. The concept may be, but in practice no.

Anyway see, I'm walking in the Mall when this guy I think is watching me. I'm stood looking in a shop window where they have these toys and lots of like cartoon characters that are mechanical. Like those crazy Father Christmases that hold their bellies and rock saying ho ho ho. Mirrored the other side I see this guy watching me. I move and I can see, he's still focused on me. So I wander casual along the Mall and stop at another window where I can see behind me and the guy is still with me so I take the escalator up a floor and as I turn at the top, I can see he's on his way up too.

I take another escalator and I'm on what they call the food court, where I don't want to be because I have no money. So I get the down escalator and he is on the up and we could almost touch. By this time, I'm starting to worry. I'm wondering whether he's from the children's department or police looking to nab me for something I ain't done or is he looking for a nice fresh faced boy where he can lodge his meat and two veg. You understand me.

Yeah, well I'm not too bad looking, there have been one or two older boys at the home who have wanted the same and I'm not giving. The thought horrifies me. One boy, Darren, I clunked with a brick, sent him to hospital because he pushed it. He never split, because well then I was only thirteen and he was going on eighteen and he would have been nailed as a paedophile the dirty sod. So I may have nice blond hair and blue eyes and pink lips, as Alexa at school told me but I'm not that way inclined.

I reach the bottom and make for the exit. Just as I get to the door, I decide to hide up and I dodge into this shop and then discover it's a girl forest, all these stands of girl stuff, skirts, dresses, flimsies, briefs and bras and god knows what else girls like to throw on their bodies and I hide up and peep through the strings of what they label 'Chemises on offer' in hand writing blue on white. I see the guy go by and he leaves the Mall. I think about it. He was defo following me, oh yeah that's absolutely certain, but why? I may be pretty, as Mohammed Ali said, but come on, I don't look that way do I? I mean I don't think I mince about or have effeminate gestures, nor am I wearing lippy or eyeliner like some guys do these days. I'm in trainers, jeans, clean but a bit worn and the crutch is nowhere near my knees, a clean white T and I remembered to brush my hair. I can't be that attractive for some poof to pursue me. So what's going on? Jesus, if a boy can't walk the Mall without being followed by some bent bastard, it's a pretty kettle.

Anyway, he's gone, whoever he was. Maybe a store detective I think, not a poofter. I walk back and I see these girls from school three of them who are always in their little gang. They are some of the nicer ones. There's Janie, I think her dad's a fireman and Sally and Kayleigh, all nice girls. At one time I was quite friendly with Kayleigh, but as I went into my shell, I sort of got left. Who bothers with a loser? Kids don't need a hard luck case to look after.

Janie waves at me and I'm surprised because in school, I'm sort of out of it, the dunce, the kid in care. I go over.

'Hi ladies,' I say. 'Don't you all look nice.' I'm not lying, they really do. I mean girls these days at my school are, well some at least, nearly as scruffy as the boys. These girls all look like new pins, sparkly, even though two are in jeans. Kayleigh wears a little skirt and I should think, twelve inches of thigh. It's a navy pleated thing and her long and perfect legs seem to reach forever down to her platform sandals. I wonder how girls dare wear what they do because there's not much covering bum and bits and yet they walk around confident and nothing shows. How do girls do that? Another great mystery that Einstein if he was still around could possibly solve. So there they stop and they look at me, quite friendly like, and Kayleigh is the first to speak.

'What are you up to Peter. No good I'll be bound.'

'Don't say that,' I say all hurt like, 'I'm just minding my own business and I think I was targeted by an arse bandit.'

'What?' They go, shocked and amused at the same time.

'You know, a paedophile. I went up the escalator to escape and he comes up after. Went up the next and so did he. I come down and we sort of pass in the middle and then he comes down and so I come down this end, making like I'm leaving the Mall and I hide in Lindy's Lingerie before I realise where I am and watch him go out the door. When I think it safe and just before the shop girl asks me if I'd like to try something, I come out and see you guys.'

'Did you want to try something?' Kayleigh asks and the three of them fall about laughing.

I now I go red and I shouldn't, should I? If I was a hundred per cent convinced boy I would just laugh.

'So what are you doing?' Janie asks.

'Nothing, mooching. I thought like to see if there were any jobs going. I got no money.'

'Is it true you're in a home?' Sally asks, sort of shy.

'Yes.'

They all sort of look like they want to ask lots of questions but don't like to.

'Why don't we go up and have a coffee?' Kayleigh says.

'I got no money, completely skint.' I say, embarrassed like. I'm the deprived kid but not yet depraved. I hope not to be. Don't let me turn out like dad, I'm thinking. Nor Mum.

'I'll stand you.' Kayleigh says.

'No you don't want to do that. I can't pay you back.'

'Doesn't matter.' I never realised how nice these girls speak, I mean like Queen's English with no South London twang. I surprise myself by saying, 'I'd like to hang with you if I'm not in the way.'

'It's up to you, like we're doing girl shopping, Claires for some earrings and hair bits and bobs and some undies and clothes and we might try on stuff but if you'll find that all too embarrassing, then you're on your own.'

'I'd like to hang.'

'Good. You can be an honorary girl. It might be an education for when you get a girlfriend. It will be interesting to see what a boy thinks too.'

'Why are you so thick at school?' Sally asks.

'Don't hold back Sal,' Kayleigh says.

'No well it's a question, because I know you're not really, I mean stupid. I guess there's something else going on.'

'He's not a thug Sally,' Jane says.

'Well I don't really get you, get where your coming from because you're not a nerd and your not a thug and you're not sporty, yet somehow you don't get bullied.'

'Well I know how to talk tough, so I suppose and I can fight dirty.'

'How?'

'Let's get those coffee's girls. What do you want Pete?'

'A medium latte if you're sure?'

'It's not a big thing is it?'

I sit and they get coffees and it takes ages to make four coffees. Eventually we are all seated and we swallow in one bite the tiny little almond biscuit thing and they are on to me again.

'So mystery man, tell us your story.'

'You don't really want to know. I expect you already heard I'm in care.'

'What do you mean? Like Council care.'

'Yes.'

'Why? Did your parents die or something?' Sally asks.

'My dad's a bank robber. He's got life, in gaol.'

'Oh Christ, sorry Pete. Do you like, visit him?'

'No I don't go near. He broke our family up, hit someone and he also kept a mistress. As a consequence, my mum is in mental hospital, well in and out and I've been in care for five years. I was fostered twice but I was trouble.'

'What do you mean?'

'The psychiatrist said I was disturbed, with my dad being in prison and mum in a home. I just hated everyone.'

'You're not disturbed now?'

'No, I've come to terms. I've got to make my own way.'

'I'm sorry, I mean we always sort of ignored you because you seemed so sulky.' Jane said.

'I was. After a time, I just learned to be alone.' I say pathetically.

'Are you still, I mean in the home?' Sally asks.

'Yeah. I'm behaving now. Keeping my nose clean.'

'It must be really hard.' Kayleigh says.

'Could've been better. Mum's the worst, just not functioning, like they've taken her brain and she used to be so bright. Anyway, I mustn't stop you having a shop.'

'Yeah let's shop.' Jane says.

'I'll see you around. Thanks for the coffee and the company.' I say politely.

'Oh you're not running away are you?' Kayleigh asks.

'Well girl shopping. It's not my scene is it? I'd be embarrassed and I'd be a nuisance.'

'Look we bought you a coffee and the condition was that you came shopping.'

'Did I agree to that?'

'By accepting the coffee, yes, that sealed the deal.'

'Oh, you're not going to embarrass me too much I hope.' I say with my best smile.

'No Petie. Would we do that girls?'

'No,' they chorused.

I hardly believe them but I have nothing better to do anyway, and they are nice girls, I mean not all girls at my school are nice in fact some are really gruesome, bullies, aggressive and physical. These girls are not. They look nice, clean, bright and fun without being loud.

'So let's go Petie.'

'I don't like Petie, doesn't sound right.' Sal says. 'Petula. Let me do something with your hair if you're going to be one of us.'

'Not one of you. Your escort.'

'Oh yeah. You're not exactly a he man are you?'

'They don't feed me properly, like Oliver Twist, stunted my growth.'

Sally was already combing my hair. I was blushing. Jane and Kayleigh sat watching with amused smiles.

'What are you doing with my hair?'

'Just a bit of restyling. Yeah there all done. Use your hand mirror to see. Oh of course you don't have one. Look in mine.' She produced a little leather folder from her cross body bag. Inside this little folder is a mirror. I move my head so I can see. I can't see much. Even that, looking in a girl's hand mirror is embarrassing. I hand it back.

But I looked and yeah she has rearranged my ample hair not that long I mean just a bit sort of over my ears and it does look really girlie. I make a move to sweep it back sort of how it was before and she stops me.

'You change it and you're not our friend, you can just go off and be boring on your own and perhaps that weirdo will find you.'

Kayleigh takes my hand. 'Come on, it's just fun. You actually look like a butch girl, a tomboy. Just a bit of fun.'

'Not if any of the other kids see me. I'd never live it down.'

'They won't so let's shop.'

So we go down the escalator and Kayleigh has my hand in a firm grip and then we walk the concourse arm in arm and even that is embarrassing because I feel that I am giving away what I really feel.

Chapter 4.

We enter H&M and they start on skirts. I try to slope off to men's wear, not because that interests me but because it's embarrassing to be in girl wear but Jane pulls me back. 'You're either with us or not. Which?'

The girls all giggle. 'OK.' I say and give my worthless opinion on mini kilts, skirt shorts, mini skirts, jeans and blouses and then they head to underwear. I follow, well I got to, under the terms of the contract I didn't sign but for sure, I'm having much more fun than I ever thought I would. I'm asked to hold items while they search for bargains. I try to look like a complete spare part, holding four mini skirts, six blouses and tops, two bras and a three pack of what looked like very brief and interesting panties.

Eventually I'm relieved of the clothes and the girls head to the changing room. The girls disappear inside, leaving me outside holding the underwear. I thought I would die of shame, but after ten minutes and the girls are still inside, I feel strong enough to endure the looks I'm given by other kids. A couple of girls my age look at me and giggle. I feel sure I blush.

At last the girls appear. 'You're still there holding the undies? I forgot to say, we don't want them. You can put them back Petula.'

'Very funny girls. Very funny indeed.' I turn to go back to the lingerie section as bidden.

'Come on, give them here,' Kayleigh says. 'I'll put them back. It was just our little joke, a tease. You'll forgive us?'

'Yes. It was quite funny. I had just got used to holding them but I was man enough to stand the looks girls were giving me.'

'Actually with your new hairstyle, I'd think everyone would have thought you a girl.'

'Not really?'

'Look in the mirror. If you just had breasts, no one would know.'

I look in the first mirror we come to.

'I see what you mean. So all the time I thought I was standing there feeling like a man holding a girlfriend's stuff, they would have thought 'why's that dyke holding those pretty undies.'

'Yes that's about it. Poor boy, we've been so cruel. Where do you live?' Kayleigh asked

'In Purley.'

'Oh that's my way Peter. Mum's picking me up, so come for high tea and then mum will run you home.'

'Are you positive? Only I have to tell the home where I am and what time I'll be home. So where will I be?'

'My house. She rummages in her handbag. 'Here's the address.' She passes a card.

'You have a visiting card?' I ask incredulously.

'Look at it. I sell cosmetics from home.' Kayleigh said proudly.

'But you're only fifteen.'

'Sixteen before Christmas.' Kayleigh tells me.

'Are you making money?'

'Oh yes. Mum helps but I'm quite well off.'

'Are you serious about going home with you?'

'Of course.'

'Then I better phone and get permission to stay out later.'

I dial and get Raymond one of the house 'fathers'. 'Raymond, it's Pete. Yes OK I know you have number recognition. I've been invited for tea. Yes of course I'll give you the phone number. And the address. Geez.' The are so bossy. I read out the address. I pocket my old Nokia.

'Thanks Kayleigh, I'm coming for tea then.'

'Good boy.'

'I'm not a dog.'

'No but you are young for your age aren't you, just a boy.'

Sally and Janie join us. 'OK you two?' Kayleigh asks.

'Spent our allowances. Were going to split. Dad's picking us up.' Sally replies.

'Oh OK.'

'So are you seeing Kayleigh home Petula?'

'Yes if she wants and less of the Petula please, it's Pete, Peter even Petie.'

'Sorry Petie, it's only you've been an honorary girl, and it was funny leaving you holding the undies.'

'Yes I guess and the hair. I can take a joke.'

'Here, kiss, moi moi. That's how we part and as an honorary girl, a temporary member, you get the same. That must be worth something.'

'Yes Jane, that's a nice benefit, but you missed my mouth.' I say being the smart arse.

'Here's to the next time.' Sally says and kisses me on the lips, not a snog just a peck, but it's lovely.

'This is what you call friends with benefits.' I say. 'I like it.'

'You kiss like a girl,' Sally says and laughs.

The girls depart and Kayleigh takes my hand just like we are boyfriend girlfriend. With her free hand, she phones her mum.

'Hi mum. I have a friend here from school. Can he come home for tea mum and then you can drop him home after? No, he's a boy. No not a boyfriend, a friend and a boy. He's all alone mum, I'll explain later. Thanks mum.' She finishes the call.

'You make me sound like an orphan.' I say.

'Well you more or less are, aren't you?' Kayleigh says

'Yes, I guess I am.'

'I can't imagine. That must be so hard. What's the home like?'

'It's OK just the people in it. Some are quite disturbed and fly off the handle at the drop of a hat. Some of the girls are on the game too.'

'What game?'

'You have lived a sheltered life. On the *game*. Meeting men for sex, and they get paid in drugs or money. The staff try and stop it but there are too few staff. The girls just go over the wall.'

'Is it rough?'

'Oh yeah, it's rough and so are some of the staff. You don't want to go there.'

'Is that why you are so quiet and like depressed?'

'Maybe. I just can't retain knowledge, like I read a page and by the end, I haven't remembered anything and then we have a test and I get four out of ten. I'm not stupid.'

'I know you're not except when standing with those undies. Now that was funny. Pete just because we found it funny doesn't mean we are against you, just like a joke on a friend.'

We emerge from the Mall and walk to Church Street and wait on the corner for her mother to arrive.

'Oh Christ there's that man who was following me earlier.'

'Where?'

'Over by the betting shop, standing in the doorway.'

'He looks harmless. Maybe it was just a coincidence that he was going to the same places in the Mall as you.'

'What up to the food floor and then down again without stopping?' I question. 'I don't think so.'

'Well here's mum, so if he wanted to talk to you, bad luck.'

We are quickly in the car and before I have found the safety belt and buckled up we are on the move because the parking wardens are really sharp her mum says.

I'm sort of introduced via the mirror, Kayleigh in the passenger seat, and I can see that her mum is a real good looking momma. I mean my mum was pretty, probably prettier, but Kayleigh's mum is attractive, groomed I think they call it. Her hair is perfect, not like glued, it moves around but it is glossy and a nice colour, light blonde I think as far as the light in the car allows me to judge. Kayleigh is also groomed for a sixteen year old. I'm in awe of them both and I wonder that a waster like me has been picked up by Kayleigh and I'm on the way to their house.

What does Kayleigh see in me? I hope this will not be another big disappointment.

Chapter 5.

We arrive at a substantial detached thirties built house, elegant with a drive that must have been thirty metres long. To me it seems a palace. My family had lived in a three bedroom social housing semi. This is definitely the other side of the tracks.

Kayleigh's mum is tall, even wearing flats she's three inches taller than me. She is also well proportioned, not willowy nor well endowed. She's blond, going towards ash blonde I think they call it and her face is like upper class, no expression of oppression or discontent. Tranquil, that's what I would call her facial features. She's a perfect example in my mind of what a mum should be, someone of whom to be really proud. Cool, loving, neat and tidy and I would hope, even tempered.

Kayleigh herself is a good-looking girl. In contrast to her mum, her hair's light mouse, but she has the same blue eyes and pleasant expression and bone structure. That Kayleigh has befriended me is a complete surprise and I had half expected her mum to turn up and say, 'be off with you beggar'. Of course she didn't, that was just me feeling inferior.

'What are you two eating?' Her mum asks. I'm so surprised. When I had a family I was never asked that. Mum cooked and I ate and she wasn't a bad cook either. Mum had married beneath her. She'd been the daughter of a bank manager, went to a grammar school, selective education and she had done well. Instead of going to Uni, she had met my dad who swept her off her feet and infected her with his happy-go-lucky lack of responsibility. There is only so long you can live such a life. Even though I'm just coming up to fifteen, I know that if you lead a casual life, it catches up and the remainder of ones life can be all the more difficult. Therefore I'm determined to be nothing like my dad. The downside to this resolution is, that knowledge just doesn't stick in my head.

'What do you want to eat?' Kayleigh asks me.

'Anything, whatever you're having.'

'Salmon and new potatoes and salad mum. That all right Pete?'

'Sure. Thanks.'

'Then you can scrub the potatoes Peter,' her mum says.

'Is dad eating with us mum?'

'No dear, he's at the club for dinner.'

'Dad does golf on a Saturday,' Kayleigh informs me. 'Now apron on Pete.'

'Is this another of your jokes, dressing me in some girlie apron?'

'No Petie, it's to protect your clothes.'

'What jokes have you been playing on him?' Her mum asks.

Kayleigh tells how I stood outside holding flimsy undies. Her mum smiles and smiles at me too. 'It's a form of affection Peter, playing a joke like that. You should feel honoured.'

'Yes Mrs Dawson I know, but I'm just on my guard with these girls now.'

'Pete is in a home mum, because he has no parents.'

'Oh that's unfortunate. How is that Peter?'

So I tell her my hard luck story and she gives me these questioning and sympathetic looks. She puts an arm around my shoulders as though I'm a little boy and to my shame, I start to cry. Look, I never cry. All the things that have happened to me like taking mum away in the ambulance and dad being arrested, I never cried. If I ever get punched at school, I never cry, just give a two for one in return and dad taught me not only how to punch but where, like in the throat or a tooth rattler to the side of the jaw.

Anyway there I'm booing in their kitchen, a potato in one hand and a scrubbing brush in the other. Fantastic impression that must make. Then to make it worse they are both wiping my tears like I'm six years old or something. Christ! I feel like running out of there as fast and far as my feet will carry me. I feel so ashamed.

They are so kind. 'It's better sometimes to let go, give in to your emotions Peter. You have been through a lot by the sound of it with no one to support you.'

Well I recover and put the potatoes in boiling water and add just a touch of salt under direction and then I'm taken into the garden and pick this leaf that they tell me is mint and it tastes like mint and smells wonderful and I put a sprig of that in with the potatoes.

'I've never done any cooking. I just learned something. It's interesting isn't, when you know how to cook something that doesn't come out of a packet all prepared.'

Mrs Dawson shakes her head. 'It's such a shame that no one is teaching you these things. Well as long as Kayleigh wants, you are welcome here. We only have her and seldom see her because she has her business. She will tell you about it after we eat, but she has taken over the third bedroom as an office and store room. She promised that she would only work on a Sunday, but it's got to be everyday. So perhaps you could help when you come round?'

'Of course.' I say. The prospect of being a regular visitor after being a loner for so long is a welcome surprise. I can hardly believe my luck.

'Petie, how would it be if I gave you some coaching in school work? You should be doing better than you are, you're a nice boy and far from stupid.' Kayleigh says, and she is the class brainiac.

'That's what I want, one to one, perhaps then my brain wouldn't drift off to thinking about mum and things.'

'So what do we need to do as far as the home is concerned?' Her mum asks.

'Just tell 'em that you are prepared to be what they call in loco parentis, responsible for me while I'm with you and they may vet you, to see you're not a paedophile.'

'I dare say we can put up with that.'

After tea or dinner they call it, like they are quite posh, so nearly everything has a different name, like serviette and napkin and of course they have them even when it's just like the three of us and of course they don't do things like eating and talking at the same time, nor do they cram the food in like a forklift truck delivering a pallet.

I try to remember the things mum taught when I was young and forget the manners of the pigs in the home. Not pigs really, just they sort of behave like them at times.

Some are a lot worse off than me and can't even remember their parents.

Anyway, I think I acquit myself pretty well. It's real nice to be there, a lovely and beautiful mum who seems really calm but who I reckon has high standards and would not put up with any nonsense and my new friend Kayleigh who is as kind as her mum, obviously clever and a beautiful girl, probably one of the top most beautiful girls in school and who most of the guys think is snobby and unattainable.

Well she may be unattainable for those little perverts, testosterone boiling in their blood stream, making dirty jokes and noises when any nice looking or not so nice looking girl comes within yards. They just want to get their leg over and boast after, but she sort of picked me up and I really appreciate that and what I feel, is a deep affection for her. I'm flattered that clever as she is, she has seen something in Peter James Wallace, even though I'm twenty third in a form of thirty-two and she is a top student.

She takes me up to her office and she shows me all these cosmetics that she sells on line, a bit cheaper than what you can get on the high street. They are she tells me all top makes, like some of the names I've seen in the shops. There's hundreds of boxes on metal shelving that has holes all over it and each is labelled up with what it is, mascaras and brow pencils and foundation and stuff, even sets of brushes in little tie cotton bags that she tells me are for applying makeup. I never knew. I mean I know about makeup because we boys laugh at one or two girls who are really over the top and come to school looking like a cross between a clown and a geisha, those Japanese girls.

She shows me the website and then the order list since the last time she opened up and there's fifteen orders at sort of average a tenner each time. That's one-fifty pounds and she tells me that her net profit on that is a third, so fifty quid in her pocket or rather, her bank. Then she has what she calls her purchase ledger and her sales ledger and hopefully at the end of each month she has more in the sales than the purchase. Then she's really crafty, because some customers sign up and get regular supplies for a five per cent off and then another thing, repeat orders get a small gift, like an eyebrow pencil. Christ, the stuff a girl needs. She tells me she is like moving into other feminine areas, like some cheaper perfumes named after pop stars who all seem to have their own what they call, fragrances. My mum called it scent. Then she surprised me by taking me in a small room and showed me boxes of real feminine stuff, tampons and other stuff that men don't want to know about. She sells that too and she says she can because the mark up is horrendous and no matter what the state of the nation, girls need these things. I had no idea there was easy money to be made

So she gets me sat down and shows me how to process the orders, producing an invoice for each. That done we then make up the orders and stick the stuff in padded envelopes with the label that has been printed with the invoice and a little note of thanks in silver writing and with a posy of flowers at the side. She checks that we also put in the free gift for the deserving and this time it's a little brush for putting on eye colour, shadow she calls it.

We just finished when her mum enters and says it's time to take me home in time for the nine o'clock curfew. I have found it all so fascinating, getting to know girl stuff and working with Kayleigh is so nice. She's a wonderful girl. I wish I could be half as, there you see, here's the admission, half as lovely and graceful.

We go down and her mum locks up and sets the burglar alarm and we get in her nice clean black car and she drives me the mile to the children's refuge.

I'm surprised when we get there because she locks the car and we all go in and she asks to see Philips, the boss and he comes out from the back. I show Kayleigh around, the pool table and the swings for the young kids out back and the table tennis and TV room and the sort of studio that has a mike so we can do karaoke. And then my room, which isn't that bad, I mean small but at least I'm not sharing like some of the younger kids. And I keep it tidy and neat and there's no underpants lying about.

'What's that smell?' she asks. And I don't need to sniff myself.

'It's eau de orphanage,' I say, 'we make it out of farts, boiled cabbage and the loo cleaner plus just a touch of the paraffin wax they use on the ground floor parquet.'

'I don't think it will sell.' She says laughing.

'We better go down and see where your mum has got to,' I say and take her hand and Barbara comes out of her room, big grumpy girl who just keeps eating and makes soppy noises because there I am holding hands with a pretty girl.

'You're wastin' your time in 'im, queer boy.' She says with that nasty smirk she has.

'Are you?' Kayleigh asks as we go down the broad staircase in this great old converted late Victorian house.

'What gay? I don't think so, just I don't sort of mix with her and her gang. I mean if I came from the wrong side of the tracks, she would be about a mile down the road to nowhere the wrong side.'

'I don't like this place,' she says. 'I'm sorry for you being here.'

'You sort of get used to it.'

We sit on this bench waiting for her mum and Kayleigh says to me, 'What if my mum doesn't ever come out. I might be stuck here.'

'No you got a dad,' I say.

'Oh yes, what I see of him. He's OK, but works hard and then Saturday is his play day, so I see him on a Sunday and most of that, unless we do something special, I'm working in the business and doing homework. Saturday is really my play day.'

Philips opens his office door and calls me in.

'What about Kayleigh?' I ask, not wanting to leave her sitting alone.

'Both of you.' He says.

So we go in and stand because there are no more seats. 'Mrs Dawson has a proposition for you Peter. She has suggested that you stay with the Dawson family at weekends, that's Friday after school till Monday when you go to school. It's an unofficial arrangement because we have to vet. How do you feel about that? If it doesn't work out, you can always spend the time here.'

'It sounds great to me but you better ask Kayleigh how she feels. I mean she's a girl and I wouldn't want to be a drag and always hanging around her neck like that albatross in that Ancient Mariner poem we were doing.'

'Well we can sort those things out as we go. I'm not saying this is forever. We will see how it goes Peter.' Mrs Dawson says. 'If you fit in, it could be good for both of you.'

'I like the idea of having a brother. Yes mum.'

'Well that's settled.' Philips says. 'They will send someone round to see you and Mr Dawson to make sure he's in good hands because we have a duty of care that we will be delegating to you. Everyone has to be happy and above all safe.'

So that's that. From next weekend, I shall be staying at Kayleigh's. I'm over that moon like the cow in the nursery rhyme mum taught me when I was little.

I go out and see them off and we kiss, first Mum kisses me and oh my god I just feel so wonderful having this lovely woman holding me and kissing my cheeks. Then it's me and Kayleigh and she is so sweet and holds both my hands and kisses my cheeks. This has been the best Saturday in living memory. I feel like crying again but I daren't because brats are watching from windows and they will have enough stupid comments and nonsense as it is. I stand and watch as they drive away and have to bite my lip so I don't cry. I can't afford to let my rep down. I'm little tough guy and no one touches me.

Barbara called me queer boy. Well that I'm not and she only does that because I don't have anything to do with her. I don't have much to do with any of them but if someone is being bullied I will bash the bully without warning. I have a reputation see?

Chapter 6.

The next school week drags by and suddenly I am getting better marks, like a history test on Elizabeth the first, I get sixteen out of twenty. The teacher looks surprised as he gives my paper back to me.

At the end of class he says, 'A word if you please Peter Wallace.'

Whether I please or not he means, and I stand there like a naughty boy while the others file out, poking me in the ribs and sort of jeering.

'How did you do that Peter?' Mr Russell the history teacher says.

'What sir?' I ask because he should clarify the question. See I have knowledge and words just can't remember when I try and study. Maybe I shouldn't study too hard.

'Eighty per cent in the test. If you keep that up you will get an A in GCSE.[2]'

'Dunno sir. My brain must have been working for a change.'

'You weren't cribbing?'

---

[2] General Certificate of Secondary Education taken in year eleven/twelve in UK.

'No sir. Sir I take that as a slur against my personal integrity. Just I'm happier sir. I think that helps me remember stuff.'

'Why are you happier?'

'I'm spending my weekends with a family, not in the home, like from end of school today and coming into school Monday, I'm living with this family.'

'Good for you. You may go. Keep up the good work and behave.'

'Sir, Mr Russell,' I say and beat it to my next class. I'm just a bit late and explain to this teacher Geography, Browning, that I had to see Mr Russell.

For the first time I put my hand up when Browning asks a question. Of course as this is a rare event in the life of me and Browning, he asks me, thinking perhaps, I'll offer something stupid as an answer to, 'Do we all know the meaning of tsunami?'

He looks around the class and his eyes settle on me like a vulture spotting carrion.

'Yes Wallace offer us a pearl of wisdom.' He says and I know he is being sarcastic.

Martin a gangly boy on the back row, clever but big headed says loudly, 'This should be interesting,' sarcastically. I hate that big bastard.

So I collect my wits and out comes the answer. 'A giant tidal wave sir, often caused by an earthquake or alteration in the earths crust. Like the one in Sumatra and Indonesia in 2004.'

'You surprise us all Dawson. A perfect answer. Come up and write the word on the board.'

'Sir?' I say, reluctant because if I go up other kids will take pot shots if I get it wrong.

'Come along, surprise us all again.'

So I go up and he hands me a dark blue whiteboard marker and I write, *tsunami* - Japanese word.

'Well done Wallace. Don't make judgements Martin. No one likes a clever Dick.' And as I return to my seat, Martin has this red face and a few kids are sniggering.

I make the flushing motion and I see him look like he wants to spit flames at me. I feel so proud that I have actually done two things good today. As I walk to the school gate, Martin tries to kick my legs from under me. He's a big farm boy, loose limbed, a rugby full back. Anyway, I avoid his kick and swing a bunch as I pirouette catching him a glancing blow on his cheek. He sways off balance and I kick him in the balls. I turn and I'm out the gate and away. I don't even look back. He leaves me alone after that.

End of the school week and I meet Kayleigh holding my battered little suitcase in my hand.

Her mum picks us up and off we go. At theirs I change into civvies and I take my school stuff down for washing.

'Can you do that?' Her mum asks.

'If I know where the washing machine is?' I say.

'Well Kayleigh has washing too so wait and it will all go in together.' She calls up the stairs for Kayleigh to bring down her stuff.

I feel funny that my boy pants and her little knickers will be circulating and dancing around in the machine together. I mean we aren't that well acquainted yet.

'Yes Mrs Dawson,' I say sort of shy.

'You can't call me Mrs Dawson all the time if this is to be a regular thing. My name is Rosalind or mum or mummy. Call me what you like but not Mrs Dawson.'

'Yes, um, Rosalind thank you.'

Kayleigh appears and she sees my few things on the floor by the washer in their laundry room and she sorts it and puts it in on a mixed wash at thirty degrees and it will take nearly three hours. After that time, my undies and hers will be well acquainted.

So then we set the table in the dining area of this open plan kitchen diner. I don't know how because in the home we just pull what we need from the cutlery box. This is all new and putting salt and pepper on the table and no Ketchup or brown sauce seems wrong. In the home we must consume almost as much tomato ketchup as we do food. Then me and Kayleigh go up and do homework and I have algebra and I don't have a clue.

I sit one side of the table and she the other and I look at this question and I can't do it. 5X = 14: What's the value of X. I'm wishing that 5X was fifteen then it would all make sense.

'Stuck? She asks and I know I'm embarrassed because although she has said I'm not thick, I am.

'Yeah.' I say and my voice has gone all husky admitting I'm an idiot. She comes round my side and puts a hand on my back and that is so comforting. 'It's pretty easy isn't it?' Think what it would be if it was 5X equals 15.'

'That would be three. Easy.'

'So as it's fourteen it will be less than three. Five into fourteen goes two doesn't it? That leaves four. Five into four won't go, so add a nought and divide by five and you get forty over five which equals?'

'Eight.' I say as though I'm a genius.

'So the answer is?'

'Well it can't be twenty eight so it must be, two point eight.'

'See you can do it, you just think you can't. Do the rest and I will see how you've done. I won't correct but I'll say if any are wrong.'

So over the next hour I do the algebra and it's like a light has gone on and it's not so hard any longer and instead of taking a stab at an answer I have worked them out. Then I have to write a short story, and I have an idea, an idea about a train accident, the train coming to a sudden stop as it hits a tractor on a crossing like I saw on TV last week and I imagine the people being thrown about and hurting and the ambulances and sirens and police and the tractor driver who got stuck on the line, he leapt for safety and sits shocked, head in hands and the ambulance staff attending him and the passengers. Then I added the spilled fuel and the fire engine hosing down and clearing up.

I'm pretty pleased. Kayleigh reads it through and finds my spelling is dismal, I spelled ambulance three different ways, each one wrong in a different way and I kept switching from present to past tense, and she explains that. I just want to hug her because she is just about the best teacher ever. I write it out again, nicely.

So that's me done except I have to read Jane Eyre by Charlotte Brontë. So far it has been a bit gloomy, especially as Jane is an orphan like me, well I'm almost an orphan. I don't know where this story is going.

Kayleigh says, 'Well, it's a love story but you have to get though the horrible bit. Why don't we watch the film and then you will have to read the book after.'

'Can't we just watch the film?'

'No because the film doesn't tell all the story and they take liberties because making a film is basically different to telling a story on the page.'

So after dinner we watch the film and it is dark. She has to battle against all sorts, a cruel aunt and horrible cousins, a young priest who wants a wife before becoming a missionary, a cruel employer who keeps his mad wife in the attic and the harsh social order of the time that kept those at the bottom servile and hopeless. Like his girl friend comes and treats Jane who is a governess, so has some standing in the household like a common servant. Yet in the end she finds happiness mainly because she is a good person. Wow, what a tale. If I could write like that.

'That was really good,' I say. 'It was like a horror film except humans were the monsters and it had a happy ending.'

'So now read the book and you will see how cleverly she puts the sequence of events together and her words.'

'I will.' And I do. Before I switch my light out I read the first two chapters that are pretty beastly about her aunt and cousins and being sent to the orphanage. Horrible times. Poor girl, poor Jane Eyre. I'm a lot happier than her or is that she. Yeah.

I sleep really well pleased that I'm not a complete dunce after all and with a really good teacher I can get back on track. I have a really good teacher because Miss Clever Clogs Kayleigh is patient and understanding and prepared to use methods to inspire and explain and help me think through a problem. I'm so grateful. I have yet to meet her dad and I guess that will be Sunday as he is Captain or something of the golf club and spends a lot of time there.

I wake in the morning and I say to myself, 'I have done all my homework, on time and out of the way.' It is such a relief and I feel proud and like a saint for doing so.

I wonder what I shall do today. I turn over onto my back and just think how lovely it is lying in a nice bed between fine cotton sheets in a room I could really swing a cat in if I was that cruel. I shiver at the thought. I hate any form of cruelty. I like cats too. They are loners like me and like me, if stroked the wrong way or someone takes liberties, they strike back. Cats are their own people not like fawning dogs.

I get up and use the guest bathroom that is apparently at my disposal, Rosalind's words. I have a quick shower and wash my hair using the shampoo and stuff that's there and clean my teeth and after I dress in what's my best, jeans and a T.

Creeping downstairs, I'm wondering if there's anyone about and I listen for sounds of movement. I go into the kitchen feeling a bit like a trespasser. There is a man sitting there and I guess he must be Mr Dawson.

'Good morning,' I say. 'Are you off to golf today Mr Dawson?'

'So you're who? I forget your name.'

'Pete Wallace.'

'Oh yes Pete, well welcome Pete. Perhaps I'll get to know you tomorrow. Just let me say, if I find anything going on with my daughter, you'll be sorry.'

'N'nothing like that. I'm just grateful to be here, really Mr Dawson. You have a wonderful daughter.'

'OK son. I said what I had too. Welcome to the house and you don't need to tiptoe around. If you're living here, even part time, then you are here on equal terms, but don't sit in my chair and, when sport's on TV, the TV is mine.'

'I get it, I mean yes sir, Mr Dawson.'

'Harry. I'm proud of my girl, proud that she has befriended you. You had it rough son I hope this helps.'

'What do you do Harry?'

'I'm a policeman.'

'What in one of those souped up BMWs?'

'Detective Superintendant, dealing with toe rags all week long. Saturday is my day of rest or recreation at the golf club where I burn off steam, Sunday is family day. Do you play?'

'No I never have. Is it as difficult as they make it look?'

'More son. If you're going to be around that long, I might give you a go. Right I'm out of here. Oh and here, I guess you could do with some pocket money. Here's a tenner. Be good.'

He gives me a look that almost freezes the marrow and then he smiles. 'I think I can trust you not to do any commuting at night.'

'What do you mean? Oh I get it. You have my word.'

'Good, well I'm off. I'll take you to the club one day Peter.'

I sit and think blimey. I wouldn't like to be a criminal. I wonder whether he knows about my dad and dad's reputation has tainted me. Jeepers I hope not. I'm not going to be a scally[3] like him. I have a year before my GCSE exams and somehow I'm going to get those passes, not just passes but at least B's. I help myself to cornflakes and juice and then I make tea for myself. I would take a cup up to Ros and Kayleigh but I don't know about visiting a lady's bedroom, I mean I've never done that and I respect their privacy. So I sit and watch the news on the TV, the same as Harry was watching, I don't even dare change the programme.

I hope Kayleigh will be down soon. I feel very alone and out of place. Oh it's beautiful here but I don't know their expectations of me, their manners are most likely not mine, brought up rough as I've been. I wish this home could have been mine.

Now I understand why Kayleigh is so finished, so brainy and smart, in mind and appearance. She has been brought up, not dragged not left to roam the streets as I have been with a drunken crooked father and a mum on pills that have taken away her love, all her emotions and her reasons to stay alive.

---

[3] Scallywag. In UK and slang in some parts for a wrong-doer, a wrong'un.

Chapter 7.

Kayleigh is last down. Rosalind enters all brightness and done up like always. I mean her dress is not spectacular but she looks altogether. She's lovely and I can smell her perfume as she sweeps into the kitchen and gives me a lovely smile.

'Hello.' I say and feel stupid.

'I'm going to see a friend today Peter, so you two will have to bus if you want to go anywhere. You will probably need money, so here.'

She proffers another tenner. I'm so tempted but I say, 'Harry already gave me a tenner.'

'Oh you met my husband? I expect he impressed on you that any sort of sexual contact with Kayleigh would not be appreciated?'

'Yes he did and I hope I reassured him and, well you too. I'm just so pleased to be here, out of the home and with a companion like your daughter. I think she's wonderful.'

'Are you in love with her?'

'Well, yes, I mean I have never had a friend like her. She's so strong and kind, not something I'm used to in one person. If you're asking whether I'm in lust, then I would say no, so don't worry, I'm not going to leap on her.'

She laughs. 'Good boy. She is a remarkable child. Are you going to help with her business, because that will free me up if you do?'

'Of course, if she wants me to.'

'Thank you. Well I'm off, so be good. Don't burn the house down.'

She went out the door and a few seconds later I heard her car start and the scrunch of tyres on the gravel. Another five and then the door opens to reveal Kayleigh looking bloody super as always. Her eyes are so big and that intense blue set against her dark hair that looks more like dark chestnut today is blooming beautiful.

'Hi. Can I get you any breakfast,' I say just for something in the way of a greeting.

'I can get it. I have some orders come in overnight. Could we do them and then take them to the post? Then we can go to the Mall and see who's about and maybe do a film. Is that your best rig, those jeans and that T?'

'I'm afraid so. The Council aren't that free with a clothing allowance.'

'Then we need to do some shopping.'

So she has breakfast and I sit and try not to stare because she's so fascinating and I wonder about her boobs in her bra and whether she feels restricted or girls just get used to that band around the chest and straps over the shoulders. I wish I could get inside her skin, just to know how she ticks, just for a day, a few hours. How she feels and what she feels and what she likes? I also wonder what she really thinks about me too? I feel so inferior to her in every way.

There's something else that worries too and I hope it doesn't show, but for about two months now, my chest hurts around my nipples and they are both swollen. I don't mind that they hurt if it is natural and I don't know and really have no one to ask. When I was lying in bed and feeling them hurt, I sort of dreamt, well I suppose it was more a day dream, that I was getting breasts and that would just be the beginning of some magic process where I would turn into a girl. I just hope that Kayleigh doesn't notice. If I am really turning into a girl, then I figure it's because I wished and kissed a frog. I really did so that shows how desperate I am. Actually kissing the frog didn't do anything for me. I wonder what the frog thought.

So we go up and I'm amazed that we have twenty-three orders. They are easy to fill. We just print the invoice that generates the label, label an envelope and then fill with goods and copy of the invoice. All the payments go through PayPal, so it's real easy. A child could do it, with a bit of nouse buying the software and setting up the site and connecting through eBay and Amazon. She looks on the computer. 'That's another seventy five in the bank.' She has checked everything I've done but I don't mind because she can't afford to make mistakes or she will get bad reviews. She is, I was going to swear, but I'll just say, really clever.

We put all the envelopes in a shopper and we hit the trail down to the main road, walking down the steep hill.

All the places around here are built up and down hills that are steep but not that high. There are a few valleys where the main roads run and the shops are, but all the residential is in steep hills. If we get a real downpour, the valley floods and the iron gratings over the sewers sometimes blow off and the motorist who takes a risk, can find himself stuck with water over the bottom of the doors.

So we dodge in the post office first and send off the parcels. Then we get the bus into the Mall.

'You need some clothes.'

'I only have twenty pounds,' I say.

'Oh well we'll see what we can get.' We start in H&M and then we go in New Look and lot's of other stores and then we go back because my clever friend has made notes and back to H&M and she buys me these nice jeans after making me try on about six pairs and it's so really embarrassing that with each pair I have to leave the changing room and go out so she can see.

After the third pair, I say, 'Look, you may as well come in the changing room, I'm wearing pants so there's nothing to see.' My pants are clean on this morning so I'll not be embarrassed by a stain or anything. What I don't want her to see is my titties.

After thirty minutes, I have a nice approved pair of new jeans and a pair of respectable shorts. We look at shirts and she says they have to be white cotton and she buys this button down collar shirt that is real preppy and another that has a V neck that I think looks real girly but she says it will show off my manly chest. I really blush at that because if she saw my breasts, she might have a fit. I don't have a manly chest, nor any man fur, I'm pleased and yet ashamed of that. Last she buys me some sneakers and some moccasins.

I'm embarrassed that she is paying and seems to think nothing of spending near a hundred pounds on a poor little orphan. 'I'll pay you back but it might take a while,' I say, 'and you better take the money mum and your dad gave me.'

'Oh you mean *my* mum gave you? That was confusing.' She says and I am burning up with embarrassment.

'Sorry I said mum, of course your mum, only she said before she went out I could call her mum and well, I would quite like to if you don't mind.'

'Of course not. I'd like you to be my sibling.'

'What's that?'

'Oh you don't know sibling. Brother or sister.'

'Oh. Thank you. I like you being my sister, makes me feel really secure. I will pay you back.'

'Yes OK. One day, no hurry. You can pay it off with the help in running my business.'

She always sounds so grown up compared to me. So then we head up to food and we decide just a cake and coffee and we will eat at home as we are fending just for ourselves, maybe get fish and chips with mushy peas on the way home.

We go to the cinema and we look at the dozen films they have on. There's about three we figure worth a watch and we debate. In the end we decide to go for Beauty and the Beast. It's an OK film. I learn she doesn't do horror nor sci-fi unless it's Star Wars. That's fine by me. I don't do horror neither, my life has been horrible enough.

We leave the theatre and make our way to the bus stop, me carrying the shopper over my shoulder with my new togs, like I seen the girls doing and that makes me feel good. Somehow I'm going to have to pay for my new clothes or as she calls it, wardrobe.

We are soon back in her neighbourhood that's smart, up market houses but down in the high street there's restaurants, Chinese, Indian, Greek, a place called Le Bistro presumably French and an Italian, to name but a few and also Charlie Ching's fish and chips. So that's what we have. Charlie is a Chinaman who always has a smile and his food is the best of the sort you can get around there according to Kayleigh. So she carries our food and we walk up the hill to her place that is about a quarter of a mile from the valley to near the top. From their house they have great views over the valley and the golf course behind to walk or run on.

We bung the food on plates and give it a twenty second blast in the microwave and in that time she produces sauces and vinegar and we eat and she's right, good fish and chips, not oily and they taste fresh.

'So what now,' she asks, putting the dishes in the washer after taking the wrapping straight out to the trash She leaves the door open to get rid of the smell.

'You might have some more orders to do.' I say trying to be supportive.

'Well they will wait till tomorrow if I have. There's nothing on TV and Dad won't be home for a couple of hours and mum, I don't know what time. I wondered,' she says coyly, 'if you'd let me do something.'

'What?' I say quite alarmed after what her dad said this morning.

'Just see what you look like if I made you up as a girl.'

'Why do girls like to do that?' I ask and I'm already blushing.

'It's fun, making a boy into a girl I suppose because most boys really hate being thought girly.'

'I don't think I'm girly.'

'No you're not, I would never think that but on the other hand you are not super boy either. You're sort of neat.'

'Neat? What does that mean?'

'Like you are really polite and sensible but not at all sissy. You walk properly, some boys walk like a chimpanzee and they sound like one. You don't. That's why I like you. It would just be fun to see you made up in a,' she stops and changes her mind about what she will say, 'well let's just do hair and makeup.'

I put my head on one side, sort of studying her, like I saw once in a film, this killer in the American Civil War used to do that as though making his mind up whether to shoot one of his own side after a disagreement. It was called Ride with the Devil with Toby Maguire as the rather naïve good guy. I thought he was, and here I'm letting you into my inner mind, really something. His voice. I'll say no more. Well, the star I really identified with was Sue Lee Shelley who played Jewel. I never told no one that.

'You really want to?' I say and it's not me talking is it, like I'm listening in surprise.

'Yes come on, it'll amuse me and I'm sure you. I'll do it properly, I don't want to make you grotesque. Pretty please?'

How could I say no, I mean this girl who has given me so much today, mind I want to pay her back and she brought me into her home. I'm so grateful for that and of course, this is a dream come true.

Before she starts I say, 'You tell no one about this, will you?'

'Why would I? Of course not Petie.'

She leads me to her room and sits me on her stool and then she does the works. She fixes my hair back with a net and I know that's a girl thing for a start. She cleans my face with a cotton pad and keeps up a running commentary, telling what she's doing and why as though she is teaching me for the future. She says I have lovely

65

skin and I need to take care of it. She shows me the pad and it has turned dirty grey, so my face was actually filthy. She starts on my eyes, eyeliner and I find that really hard, trying not to blink.

'I'd really like to pluck your eyebrows,' she says. 'Still we can do that another time.' I wonder about that, I mean if it was noticed at school my life would not be worth living. At the same time, I want her to do it. A yearning that I have buried for so long is bubbling to the surface, like too much detergent in a wash and the bubbles just keep multiplying, so this long buried, hidden desire is taking me over.

She does mascara, and I try to look amused rather than frightened but there's a little part of me that wants to investigate, my feminine side, to find out what girls get out of all this and whether I really like it? As she progresses I'm becoming more and more excited and when she turns away, I have to subject my penis to some treatment, forcing it down and trapping it down, restricting the blood flow.

She adds some subtle eye shadow and tells me what she's doing and the product as she calls this stuff, she is using. Finally she applies foundation and lips and blusher but subtle so I don't look like a demented clown. All the time she studies me as though I'm a canvas, not a person and I can't see in the mirror because she has turned it around.

Lastly she brushes my hair and I just love that and when she is doing that she sort of caresses my nape, which is lovely. Mum used to do that when I was young and she was still mum.

'There,' she says, that's you in makeup. Can I get you to dress as well?'

'That wasn't in the bargain.' Male pride is still there, the learned, conditioned reflexes that are partially instilled in boys from a young age and are partially natural instinct, to be male and proud to be so. I haven't dressed in girl clothes after dad threatened to bash me if I did it again. I was only six or seven.

Do I confess to reading mum's magazines and looking at her catalogues and loving the feel of her clothing? I cannot. Not yet, maybe never. I am so tempted.

'No, it wasn't but you look so good, no don't look yet. Look here's some stuff,' she has pulled a skirt from her rail with a blouse. Next comes a bra and panties.

'Oh no,' I say, 'not underwear!'

'Otherwise it won't look right.'

'In any case, I don't know how a bra goes.'

I know it's a lame thing to say because any idiot knows that it has a band, two cups and two straps. I don't want her to see I have these swollen breasts.

'Put the panties and the skirt on, just for me and then I'll do the rest. I'll sit over there, back turned.'

'Must I?'

'Yes please Petie. It will be so amazing to see you.'

I can't say no because I love my new sister and because I really want to. This really is my daydream come to life. 'I guess I owe you. Go on then.' I would like to tell her that this whole process has been a dreamed desire but I am too shy to tell. In doing this I am going against all my dear father tried to instil in me that boys are manly and tough and girls a bit silly, bubbly, weak, heads filled with trivialities. Yet since being with Kayleigh, no that's a lie always, I am comparing myself to girls and now to her, measuring myself, my arms, legs, hip, skin and hair texture to her. I look at a girl and want to be that girl. Real boys, men look at a girl and want sex.

'So off with your pants and put the knickers and skirt and be careful, we don't want you displaying your bits.'

'Well how do I do that? It's always puzzled me how girls can walk about in such short skirts.'

'This one is not that short. Go on.' And she walks away and I strip and I'm sort of excited now to see just what sort of a girl I make. I take off my bottom half and put on the pants and the skirt and I don't know whether the zip goes to the side or the back or even the front. Girls seem to have no rules about dress. 'OK,' I say when I'm ready and my face burns.

'Well nice legs. I bet they would look gorgeous in tights.' She turns the skirt so the zip is at the back. 'The label always goes to the back.' She says imparting some essential girl knowledge.

She pulls my top carefully so I don't spoil makeup or get lippy all over the clothes. To her direction, I put the bra on and she hooks it up. I was wondering wasn't I, if girls notice that around their chest and I certainly did. She stuffs a hankie in each cup.

'Petie, you have breasts.'

"I haven't.' I say quickly, defensively, denying what I would dearly love because of a sense of shame.

She unbuttons the blouse and I slip that on and she does the little buttons. She fastens a bracelet around my wrist.

'Petie, I couldn't help noticing, you do have breasts. Did you not know?'

'Yes, I hoped you wouldn't notice. They have been there a couple of months. They don't seem to be getting any bigger.'

'I wonder why? Have you investigated.'

'No, I just thought it was a puberty thing and would go away.' I lie because I really hoped they would stay.

She looks at me critically. 'Hmm,' she says, 'Petie, you really are a boy aren't you? They really look like budding breasts.'

'I am a boy.' I'm so embarrassed.

'Have you seen a doctor?'

'No.'

'Why ever not?'

'It's embarrassing.'

'Well that's a bad reason for doing nothing. Girls face embarrassment all the time. We'll look on the web. I mean you have got boys bits?'

'Yes.'

'OK.'

Now I'm seriously destroyed. I mean a girl questioning if I have boy bits and here I am in full makeup and girl kit, a blouse and a skirt. I bite my lip but her thoughts are elsewhere.

'I wish we had shoes, perhaps mum's will fit. Don't peep yet. I want us to do that together.'

She goes and returns in a flash and makes sure I haven't peeped. She puts these heels on my feet and they just about fit. 'Right stand up and walk small steps, no not that small you're not a Chinese girl with bound feet. There you go but feet closer together. Boys tend to roll from one foot to the other, except Mrs Thatcher did that and so does Theresa May. It must be a powerful woman thing.' She watches as I go again. 'Better, in fact that is quite good, and follow me.'

We go in her mum's room and there are mirrors there so you can see side and back. I look and I see a reasonable looking girl.

'Oh my God. Let me out of here.' I say.

'You look good, don't you? I mean if we had plucked your eyebrows it would have been better.'

'Do you really think I look OK, I mean if I walked down the street, would I pass or what?'

'Oh you actually like your new image don't you?'

'No I'm just asking after you tell me I look good, how good? Would I pass say in the Mall?'

'Next Saturday we could try it out, see if you pass.'

'Not if your mum is around.'

'She won't be. On Saturdays dad golfs and mum sees her sweetheart. That's why you are a godsend, company for me. That's partly why she agreed to have you in the first place, then she found she really liked you.'

'Oh gosh.' I blushed at the news that her mum goes off to see her lover. It all seemed so matter of fact. 'How do you feel about that? Have you met her lover? Is he nice?'

'So many questions, just like a girl. Boys never seem to want to know anything except about sport. Mum's lesbian, you know, girls. Girl on girl.'

'Doesn't that all upset you?'

'Well I still have a mum and a dad. They don't fight, not in front of me anyway. Dad has a flat in London and I think he has a girlfriend there permanently. It's a marriage of convenience and they stay together for me. I have to be grateful for that. Why would mum being lesbian upset me? It's a normal part of human behaviour. Anyway, let's not talk about it. How do you feel?'

'Silly.'

'Why?'

'Well dressed as a girl.'

'So do all girls feel silly then?'

'I'm a boy dressed as a girl and that's not normal is it?'

'So all those thousands of trannies and transgender and transsexuals are abnormal are they?'

I had to think about that. 'I don't know, you are too clever for me.'

'What if I dressed as a boy, would that be abnormal?'

'No one bothers about what girls do.'

'So if I dress as a boy and go into a men's loo what would you think?'

'I'd think you mad because most men's loos are dirty and smelly.'

She laughs. 'You may be right there. You keep looking in the mirror. You like yourself as a girl don't you?'

'It's a surprise, a shock. I mean I'm just a simple boy who hasn't ever thought about being a cross-dresser, nor about trans people.' I'm ashamed that I have lied. 'Well that's not quite true. Well I mean I have sort of thought about it, but decided I'm stuck with how I was born and I had enough problems. I'm normal.'

'Oh back to that again. Normal. But then you say, you have thought about it. I think there's a bit of denial

73

going on. Sexuality and gender don't go hand in hand, they are both a continuum, like superman at one end and the gayest gay man the other for example, but in between there are all sorts, bisexuals, asexuals, transsexuals and none of them are alike. They all get wrapped up in the transgender bundle, LGBT but that just means they are not cisgender and hetero.'

'You lost me. I don't know asexual for a start.'

'Without sex. Someone who just lives without lusting after anyone else or wanting sex.'

'And what's cisgender?'

'Happy in their natal sex. Like I'm a girl and enjoy being a girl. That doesn't mean I want a boy to fuck me. You can be cis and gay or lesbian or hetero. I suppose you think that normal is like dad, fucking his bimbo all week and coming home to us?'

'No. My dad played away too. I think that's what pushed Mum over the edge, then she became dependent on counselling and psychiatry and descended to be a dependent wreck, hardly a person anymore. Are all men like that, playing away? On the whole I don't like men, don't like the male teachers because they have consigned me to the dump and don't care. The ladies are much nicer, they at least try to get me interested.' I falter, a bit. Tears are not far away. Emotionally I'm in tatters, just most of the time I manage to control everything.

'Oh Pete, sorry this was just meant to be a bit of fun. I didn't mean to upset you.'

'That's OK. Just I feel pressured and there are things I can't deal with. I'm going to get this off.'

'Can I just have a photo? You look so good.'

'What and then it gets posted on social media? I don't think so. I thought you were my friend.'

'I am your friend and I may tease but I won't betray you, not about this, dressing up or anything serious. This is just a bit of fun and I would never post it on the Web. But you do look lovely as a girl.'

'Lovely?'

'I think so yes, lovely.

'Are you serious?'

'You look lovely. Not like Vogue cover or anything, but the sort of girl I would really like to be friends with.'

I'm really frightened with each word that somehow I'm being sent into a sexual fantasy and I'm discovering things about myself that bring back memories from years ago when I was just an innocent joyful kid. Life had been hard and just being Pete in a dysfunctional family and then in a home, had taken all my thoughts and energy. I mean we all fantasize don't we, but somethings are just fantasy, like a girl dressing as a nun or a boy dressing as a grotesque woman. I have dared to think, dared to wish I had been a girl, even that I was a sort of girl and that I would magically transform like a butterfly from the chrysalis, but all that is a dream. I know about transsexuals or as they now say, transgender people. They are more and more in the news and in documentaries, but most of the ones I see are not natural looking and they are a bit weird, with tattoos and piercings and not like I imagine I would be at all. I would like to be like Kayleigh, pretty, feminine, a girl that would be described as wholesome. She is my ideal.

I study my image in the mirror. 'That's the most frightening bit. I quite like looking at myself and I can hardly believe that the she in the mirror is actually me.'

'Would you like me to clean your face with makeup remover?'

'Yes I think so.'

Kayleigh produces cotton pads and remover. She wipes my face gently and gradually Pete reappears, and yet I can still see the girl I was five minutes ago.

'There,' she says as if to a child after bathing a grazed knee, 'all better and back to normal. You go and change. Have a shower and put your dressing gown on and we'll watch a video.'

So that's what I do and we cuddle up on the settee and it's so good to have real human contact. We both smell nice too, yet I'm really frightened. She has awoken in me impulses and desires that I have too long buried. I had put them down to my dysfunctional home and lack of motherly love. She revived old joys that I had forsaken, of dressing in mum's clothes when I was so much younger and of dad's anger and the furious row that ensued.

It was after that that he taught me to as he called it, 'rough house', striking the telling blow that disables an enemy before they have time to annihilate you.

We watch a soppy film and it's really nice. I go to bed feeling so happy and yet there's a cloud hanging there in my mind.

Chapter 8.

Sunday morning and I hear voices as I lie in bed. They are the voices of a married couple discussing something, quietly and sanely and yet I find it disturbing, that they both have these other lives.

What is normal? I no longer know. Yesterday's dress up has really discomposed me. That I could also look like a passable girl, at least I thought I did, had really upset my little tough guy image of myself, the carapace I hide behind, the kid that doesn't care, the hard nut that floats alone. The kids in the orphanage would really have a ball if they knew.

Dad had taught me to be tough like him and he was only small but a well-placed punch to the throat or a kick in the balls, followed by a punch to the side of the head and the fight can be over in seconds. I had demonstrated the skill once or twice at school, and once in the home with a particularly nasty piece of work, that every one considered would turn to serious crime. After that the bullies left me alone. Nasty boy Craig treated me with respect and put his hand over his throat when he saw me.

'Oright Pete?' He would say.

'You?' I would reply.

'Still looking for my Adam's apple.'

My door is knocked and I say, 'Come in,'

Kayleigh appears and bounces into my bed. 'Should you?' I ask.

'We are not doing anything. Just I wanted to see how you are today, after you know, yesterday and making you into my sister. I'm sorry, it was just fun and I had no idea it would upset you. You won't tell mum?'

'Are you kidding? It's just dad brought me up to be a mini him, small but tough and to see myself as a girl, was so far from how things were when they were good at home.'

'I had no idea you had all these hang-ups. You always seemed so cool, the cool loner, everyone's friend but friend of none, sort of like an island. You did make a lovely girl though.'

'That's what really bugged me. Don't ask me again, because I won't do it. What do you get out of it anyway?'

'Oh that's a question. First off I have never done that to anyone before. I wanted to see the power of makeup and how it could change a face and perceptions. I look at you and I see boy, but yesterday, I saw a girl and it wasn't the clothes, it was you, your face and hair and if you had been wearing those new jeans and that boy shirt, it would have still been a girl standing there. I think, no I better not say, it would be unfair. So there we are. Anyway time to get up. We are going to Sussex, all of us, so I guess shorts for you and that V neck I bought and shoes. Would you like me to do your makeup?'

I look alarmed.

'I'm just joking. See you soon. Oh and you haven't a costume have you? In case we swim. Dad's wouldn't fit and my bikini bottom wouldn't look right unless of course you wore the whole bikini? Just a thought.' She laughs and I know she teases, but she knows not what she does. 'I expect we can pick up boys swimmers anywhere down there.'

'You do gabble on.'

'I do with you Petie. I feel really close to you. I'm really glad you're here, otherwise......'

She just stops talking and I see tears.

I pull her to me and cuddle her, and then we kiss and blimey, I'm so aroused, she is really sweet and I now think yesterday was just a bit of fun and no longer feel threatened that my feminine side will assert itself.

It's my turn to be the grown up and hug a distraught child. She recovers and smiles. She places a hand on my swollen breast.

'I looked that up,' she said, 'it's quite common in pubescent boys. It doesn't mean you are changing into a girl.'

'Oh,' I say. I'm disappointed. I mean I never seriously thought I was changing into a girl, but at the same time, I fantasised that I might. I know now, I don't want to be a boy. I wish I could be her sister.

'Thanks for the cuddle, Petie. I adore having you here, I really do. I will upset you at times I expect and you me, but we must never let some petty argument split us.'

'You are usually so together. What's brought this on?'

'Time of the month probably and yesterday seeing you as my sister and thinking I had really upset you, and mum and dad, how they are. Everything is all mixed up. I'll be fine now. Have you done all your homework?' She asks.

'Just maths to do.'

'We best get up see what the parents are going to treat us to down in Sussex and sometime we have to get that homework done, well you do it and I'll help if needed.'

'In the car, I can do it in the car, at least think of the answer in my head.'

'Good boy.'

'Woof,' I reply, 'woof, woof.'

'Funny,' she says and she has gone.

I wash and dress and I'm down before Kayleigh and mum and dad are sat at the table having done grapefruit and porridge. They are silent, drinking coffee and reading the Sunday paper.

'Hi,' I say. 'If we're going to the seaside, I need a costume because I haven't one.'

'We'll pick one up. Let me look at you Peter. Traces of makeup. What have you been up to or was it her.'

'It was her, she wanted to see what sort of a girl I made.'

'What sort of girl did you make Pete?' Her dad asks.

'Actually I might have dated myself,' I say and laugh.

'Why is it that cross dressing so amuses? Some of my coppers can't wait to get a dress on at a tarts and vicars party. Mostly they look grotesque. If they look good, I wonder about them.'

'So did she make you look pretty,' Rosalind asks and all the time I feel my face starting to burn up. I decide to not answer her question.

'Why do girls like doing that to boys?' I ask her

'That's a study for psychology students I should think. I don't care what you two get up to but what I said yesterday, I meant.' Mr Dawson says.

'Peter,' her mum says, 'Would you like to live here permanently? If I can get permission? You two get on so well and you're a nice boy, I hate to think of you in a home.'

'I would if that's OK, just I don't want to be in the way and well, there's money to think about. I mean I'm cheap to run but still an expense.'

"But the council would pay us to have you, four or five hundred a week at least.'

'Oh gosh really? Then yes, if I'm not here as a beggar and if Kayleigh wants a full time brother.'

'Well here she is. Kayleigh how would you feel if Peter was here full time?'

'Fine mum. We get on so well don't we?'

'Yes,' I said, thinking I'm not sure, after last evening when it was like having a bullying older sister. At the same time, looking back on that evening if I didn't have hang-ups, I could have enjoyed being a girl for an evening much more. I wish I could be honest even honest with myself.

'Yes we do,' I say again. 'She's a great slightly older, bossy sister.'

'Then that's what I'll tell the Children's Department.'

Kayleigh is at my side and hugs me. 'My brother. We get on well don't we?'

I nod.

'So what did you do to him last night?' Ros asks.

'What do you mean?' Kayleigh asks.

'Well he has traces of makeup.'

'Oh that, I just practised makeup on him and,' she laughed, 'he so looked like a real girl. It was fun wasn't it Pete.'

'You thought so. I felt daft.'

'Yes mum he did protest and he was a bit sulky but he was such a pretty girl when he smiled.'

'Kayleigh sometimes you are a little overpowering. Don't take advantage of his good nature. So do you really want to be fostered here, even adopted if it works out?'

'Yes please Rosalind.'

'Good. Now you are both of an age when you can act responsibly so make sure you do.'

We did. For the next three weeks I'm only there at the weekend and then the papers are signed to make them my official foster parents. I say goodbye to the children's home. I've been there much too long.

Suddenly I'm flush because from the money my new parents receive for fostering, I have fifty a week pocket money. I'm ecstatic. Life has never been this good. Mum Ros orders me to put twenty pounds a week into a savings account.

My school marks improve because my new sister who's a brainbox, has the patience and the skill to teach and because I'm now happy, my memory and powers of concentration return. Life is good in this outwardly so respectable household but in which Rosalind and Harry go their own ways. The family is dysfunctional in all but name except that they look after their daughter who still has her real parents under the one roof at least some of the time. Then I think well dysfunctional by what standards? Everyone is happy, that's what counts.

I become Kayleigh's constant companion and brother. Sometimes she's weird and spiteful, but most of the time she's really nice to me. Well no one can always be nice, not really. Some seem to be able to hide their bad moments but that doesn't mean that they never have evil thoughts. Kayleigh always behaves just as she feels. I find her a loving companion with moments of fire when she doesn't get her own way.

I help with her company and I'm quite able to process orders and get them ready for dispatch, while she attends to the rest, the tax forms, researching new products and changes to the web site. There's no doubt my 'sister' is a genius and like Richard Branson who started in his garage I believe, she'll go far.

After that first session when she more or less forced me into cross-dressing, she's made no further attempt to do so. I presumed that she'd done that and it was in the past and of course her mother had given her a mild reprimand. I just hope she will ask me again. I will act reluctant but since then I feel I'm becoming girlier, I mean I know I am. It's s thin line to tread being a boy but feeling I should be a girl. I have these impulses to display my femininity and yet I know the danger that will leave me in.

Nearly every Friday as soon as we are home, her mum disappears to be with her sweetheart, as Kayleigh expresses it. It was not until we were into the second half of the school summer term, that she told me that her mum's lover, sweetheart, was not just another woman but an actress. (I know one should say actor or the ardent feminists will burn me at the stake). That doesn't make any difference to her or us I should say. As far as Kayleigh's concerned, so she tells me, she's just glad that her mum has someone. She Googles and shows me photos of the actress, Davina Mcleod. She's a beautiful, svelte woman with long dark hair and elfin features. I can understand falling for such a creature, especially when I look at Rosalind's husband, the rough tough detective preoccupied with sport.

Then comes the terrorist activity in London. After years of comparative peace, when police and security services have congratulated themselves on their success in arresting these stupid criminals before they commit another appalling act, there are three atrocities in a row. Her dad works all hours and doesn't even find time for golf.

Rosalind takes off on a Friday night and reappears Sunday in time to take us out for Sunday lunch. Thus she and Davina have two nights together and when we Google again, we find Davina has been to this opening and that and lurking in the background is Rosalind. They look good together.

Our normal timetable is that her mum picks us up after school on a Friday and drops us home with money for a takeaway and then she is straight off to London to Davina. It's rather sweet I think. Everyone is happy, her dad with his girl in London all week, playing golf at the weekend, except now he is working all hours on raids and intelligence. Mum is in London too having a ball at events with Davina and we two are content to do our own thing.

I have found that Kayleigh is sober. There is plenty of drink, alcohol in the house but we don't touch it and we know kids at school who can and will supply drugs, but we shun them too.

That doesn't mean we don't have fun. The two of us are given tickets to a well known theme park with accommodation and off we go for the weekend, arriving late Friday night and returning Sunday, staying at the park hotel. We have a brilliant time. We sleep in the same bed in our twin room and cuddle and we kiss. It is bliss. I think I love my sister and it's just lovely to wake in the morning and find her beside me. We kiss good morning and then lie sort of intertwined without doing 'it' looking at each other and chatting.

The rides are fun, but being together, holding hands, cuddling and sharing a joke as we eat a piece of pizza in the park itself, is better than any ride.

The next Friday we arrive home and I sense she is in a mood. She gets snappy and when she's like that I get hurt and a bit sulky. Maybe because I come from this awful background, I'm emotionally frail. I just want to curl up, hands over my ears when there's bad temper. I can't deal with it.

We come in and we are making some tea and I drop a pan and she turns and says, 'You fucking stupid clumsy boy. When will you do something right?'

This time I actually cry and she relents and comes and cuddles me.

'Shush darling,' she says into my ear. 'I'm so sorry.'

'Why?" I ask, 'Why do you say those things. I'm not stupid nor am I clumsy.'

'No you're not my darling. Hush. Don't cry beloved. I do love you, really love you, only I just wish you were a girl. I'm lesbian like mum. That's why we haven't done anything.' She kisses me on the lips, sweetly and wipes my tears with her tongue. 'You are so sweet. You would make such a lovely girl. It's such a shame. I feel so denied.'

'I don't understand you,' I say and I'm really puzzled. 'I'm a boy and you love me you say and yet you don't love me as a boy?'

'I do but that time I dressed you, it was like, wow, I was bewitched. I wanted to romp nude with you, perhaps do something really risky, like go out onto the [4]Downs, find a hollow, and strip down, but you would still have boy bits so it wouldn't work.'

I don't know what to say. I'm glad she loves me. That means so much. 'I love you, that's why I get so upset

---

[4] The Downs are a range of chalk hills south of London, nearly a thousand feet at the highest point. The North Downs run for nearly 100 miles from West Surrey east far into Kent. The South Downs run parallel to the coast thirty miles to the south of the North Downs.

when you say those things, but I love you as a sibling should.'

'Not sexually?' She asks and I'm stunned. I don't know what to say. I think of that film I saw, oh I remember, it was 'Lonesome Dove' and this prostitute in this hotel in the middle of nowhere, a beautiful girl, played by Diane Lane falls for a real bad lot, but the rough cowboys ask her for a 'poke'. It sounds lewd, but the film was so well written that it seemed sweet, natural and yet they were using this poor girl and she expected to be used, even abused. Robert Duval looked after her and he was such a lovely man, sexy but gentle. When he died in the film, I cried buckets.

In that second, I would do anything for Kayleigh. I love her so much, I would walk through fire to rescue her.

'I love you.' I say.

'Truthfully, even though I'm lesbian?'

'Yes of course, that doesn't make any difference does it. The trouble is, I'm a boy.'

She shoves everything including the smoking frying pan to the back of the stove and turns off the elements. She turns and faces me, her back against the counter. She has that peculiar look on her face again, her snake eyes that is like a sci-fi movie and I expect beams from her eyes to penetrate my brain.

'Will you dress up for me. I'll make you so pretty. Please and we can spend all day tomorrow as two girls, even go in the Mall, if you dare? I would love to walk the Mall with you as my beautiful girlfriend.' She has her arms about my waist and has pulled me to her and she caresses my lips with hers. Her hand moves to the nape of my neck and pulls the short hair and strokes and I moan without knowing I am.

'There darling, there, I know you love that don't you. You are so sweet, even as a boy. I don't believe you are a little tough guy at all. You are quite feminine in some ways, naturally graceful, beautiful, gentle. Please do this for me.'

'OK,' I say hardly knowing what I'm doing except something has snapped in my brain, some memory or emotion from many years ago, has shot through my brain like a lightning bolt hitting a steal pylon I once saw and even though we, mum and I were at a distance, the following thunder a split second behind was like a whip crack but one thousand times louder, so that mum and I dropped to the ground, her bag of shopping and the oranges and apples from the farm shop spilling across our country lane. We were both so shocked we cuddled and wiped tears. I'm shocked now. I want to dress as a girl, I even want to risk the Mall.

Her face has lit up. 'You will? Be my girl for the weekend?'

'Well I think mum will be home on Sunday,' I say.

'No, she said Monday. They are going to a do, a TV thing, award ceremony. Mum told me while we were waiting for you to come out of school. Dad won't be home, not with the emergency.'

'So you want me to be a girl all weekend?'

'Yes please.' She kisses me on the lips and I have this desire to please her and also enjoy the excitement of being this fantasy female. She takes my hand and we go up to her room.

She starts to undress me and I say I can do that, but no, she wants to rid me of my boy clothing.

Soon I'm in the altogether, even my pants are gone. 'Go and pee,' she orders, 'and we sit not stand, and wipe after.'

I do as I'm told. I feel bewitched, excited, enjoying being her slave, being at her command and becoming this other person, this rather pretty, well, attractive girl.

I return and find she has this little girdle for me to struggle into.

'Where did you get that?'

'It's a sample, a firm suggested that I also sell rather sexy foundations and other things for trannies.'

She stands before me and gazes into my face but her hand is on my privates and she pushes and my gonads disappear and I wonder whether I will ever see them again, then she tucks Willy between my legs and pulls the girdle up tight. How does she know how to do this? I guess it's on YouTube.

'Look in the mirror, no boy bits. You are almost a girl. I want you to wear tights. First I'll put your brassiere on. You will have to learn how to do that yourself.' She kisses me on the mouth, this time wantonly, open mouthed and plays with my tongue. She adjusts the bra and places hankies in the cups.

'Look now! Did you ever see such a sweet girl?'

She helps me pull on tights, careful not to snag them and then a dress, her pink silk she had worn last Christmas to the pantomime, she told me. It feels delicious against my skin. I can't say it doesn't, even against my nylon covered legs, when I move to the dressing table. She works on my face and in fifteen minutes or so, there I am, a girl of sorts, pretty from the outside even though underneath I am still a boy.

As I gaze into the mirror I have a moment of vanity, loving the image I see there. I hold the skirt out to one side and it rustles and falls about my legs again, and the air within the skirt, caresses my skin. I look at my bare arms. She fastens a bracelet around my right wrist and removes my watch, replacing it with a small one with a diamante surround and fake silvery pink snakeskin band. I look at my lips, light fuchsia, pouty and full.

She hasn't finished. She paints my nails that same pink, and sprays me with her perfume. 'We need to buy you a couple of pairs of girl shoes, some flats and some wedge sandals, oh and I would love to see you in stilettos. How do you feel?'

I hardly know what to say. I'm in love with her, she has been so gentle with me and loving and I'm in love with what I see in the mirror. I love the feeling of the clothes that are confining and yet, liberating. I have never felt like this, even when we slept together. I bite my lip. I know this is my fate. With each day living with her, I'm more envious of her, her body, the way she wears and can play with her hair, her clothes and how she is seen by others. I want to be like her. I have always wanted that but being here and her games of dress up just confirm the feelings I have always possessed.

'Don't cry, you will spoil your makeup.' She is playing with my hair and tries something different, making my hair asymmetrical and fixing with a barrette. 'Tomorrow we can get your ears pierced.'

'But that's permanent, I mean no good having it done, I would have to keep them in.'

'We can do plain gold or little crystals. Lots of stars have them these days. Lewis Hamilton for one.'

'Do I look OK? I mean would I pass as a girl?'

'Oh do you? What do you think?'

We both stare into the mirror. Two girls stare back, heads close together, faces smiling. Oh god I love it. We get our mobiles and do selfies, the two of us, heads close and looking pretty and happy. We study the photos.

'Well do you pass?'

'I think I do, I would.'

'Yes my darling Summer. You look divine Summer. Come, I'll cook while your nails dry. Tomorrow we are catching the bus to the Westgrove Mall, where we are not known. It will be such fun.'

'What go out as a girl? Isn't that risky?'

'You can't try on girls' things if you look like a boy. We are going to have the best girly day ever. I shall have to stand guard over you because, I bet someone will try and pick you up.'

'Oh God that is frightening.'

'I'm looking after you girlfriend.'

'This is so weird. Must I do this for you? Can't you just love me as a brother.'

'Are you really happy as a boy? I don't think you are. I have seen you looking at girls' things. You are crafty and you look at them like a girl uses her eyes when you think you shouldn't take an interest. You don't turn your head but I see your eyes have looked sideways at girls' fashions in the shop windows. You never look at boy stuff. Even mum said, you are not very boy for your age, when dad was worried about what we might get up to.'

'I admit, I am fascinated by girls and yes, their pretty clothes and manners.'

'There, see I was right. Now tell me you love how you are now, in a pretty dress and looking divine.'

I bite my lip and nod, and look away. It's true. 'I do feel wonderful.' I have in that second betrayed my masculinity.

'You know, the language you use is like more girl than boy. For a start, you talk not grunt and your voice is sort of high for a grunting teenage boy.' She leaves the stove and whatever she is preparing and comes and puts an arm over my shoulders and kisses my cheek. 'Mustn't spoil your makeup. Perhaps in bed tonight, we will kiss properly.'

We eat dinner. She has made cheese omelettes with new potatoes, asparagus and spicy fried tomatoes. After, we have ice creams and then we watch 'the Devil Wears Prada'. I love the film and the clothes the girls wear, especially Ann Hathaway's costumes. I love that Ann metamorphs from a slob into a fashion icon.

As I sit with her arms around me I wonder how on earth I got into this and what my future will be like. I am realist enough to know that my World has changed forever. I have admitted something that I have known, no perhaps not known, but a lurking longing, a fascination with girls, like I am a moon to their earth, pulled in their direction even though dad raised me to be little tough guy.

So this girl, my 'sister', has not perverted, she has merely aroused in me something that was long buried. I mean with parents like mine, there was no room for a transgirl, was there? I think dad would probably as he would have said, punched my lights out and mum, well she was forever when I think about it, only a couple of yards away from using the carving knife to slash her wrists. On one occasion she had overdosed on paracetamol. Luckily, her stomach revolted against the drug before the pills did lasting damage to kidneys and brain.

We go up to bed and I'm to sleep in her room in her large bed. She teaches me how to remove my makeup and then gives me one of her nighties to wear and we are in bed and cuddled together. She takes my hand

and places it on her thigh and teaches me what she likes and how to bring her to a climax. All the time she kisses and caresses me.

Eventually we fall asleep. I wake in the night and feel the nightie and I'm so happy. I just wish as I have always wished, to be a girl, not for her but for me.

Chapter 9.

In the morning we showered together, even though I have this thing, this penis and the rest of the ugliness and it doesn't react. We wash each other and kiss in the stream of water. Today she uses some product on my hair and scrunches and blows it dry and I have a head of curls and look like some 1920s vamp especially after she has done my makeup. No silk dress but a mini that I shall have to be really careful in unless I want to be arrested for indecency. It's crinkled chiffon in a jungle pattern, ferns on a light grey green background. She has put with it, a black top that is ever so feminine. I am wearing tights again too and some pumps of her mums borrowed until, Kayleigh says, 'you have your own darling. My gorgeous girl.'

I have to try doing makeup, not too much, because she says, 'you have lovely skin, too good for a boy.' All the time she is watching and advising.

I do eye liner and then a very subtle blue bell that she says matches my eyes and mascara and I have to apply to each several times until she is satisfied. I do foundation, just a small amount from a bottle she hands me that is a stock sample. She advises to do this last in case mascara or liner goes astray. Lastly a lip liner that she does for me and leaves me to fill in with a natural lipstick.

I can hardly breathe and have to make myself take deep breaths. She applies some product to my hair that will calm down the curls a bit. The result is, that I hardly recognise myself.

'Oh what a girl you are. How do you feel?'

'Excited.' I say, not wanting to say lovely or pretty which are words applied to girls and I am still boy enough to fear having those words applied to me.

'Yes but what else, how do you look?'

"I can't bring myself to say.' I bite my pink lip.

'Never do that, you get lippy all over your teeth. How about saying you look pretty?'

'I ....I look pretty.'

'No you don't darling, you look beautiful. I've had my eye on you for ages at school, wondering, thinking you lovely then and now beautiful and there were certain things you did that made me think there was a girl inside somewhere, like you always sat knees together and you had this grace and smile. I was right, but you were so shy. You do like what you see in the mirror?'

'Yes.' My voice is husky with emotion.

'Well, then we won't do breakfast unless you are really hungry? We'll have coffee and a cake in the Mall. I'll ring for a taxi.'

Twenty minutes later we are sat in a Skoda and on our way. We sit in the back and hold hands. The driver is trying to flirt with us.

'Are you sisters?' He asks.

'Do we look like sisters?' Kayleigh replies a bit snootily.

'Well but for the hair, but then hair can be any colour you make it, you girls. There's a likeness. Best looking girls I've driven this week. So sisters is it?'

'In a way we are, lesbians in the sisterhood.' She says wickedly.

I want to die then and there. But that has shut him up until we get to the Mall. Kayleigh pays the driver and we walk in, arm in arm, my cross body bag bobs against my abdomen. I am so nervous I'm actually shivering and she feels it.

'You are OK? Really I won't let harm come to you. Now what are we going to do first? Coffee and cake?'

'Yes, I think that would be nice.'

She pulls me to me into this coffee house and pushes me before her to the counter. 'I'll have that cake and a latte darling. You get them and I'll find a table.'

I'm left standing in the queue and realise that I have to order as a girl and I want to sound like a girl too. Oh talk about being thrown in the deep end. I want to run and I'm sure I start to sweat and I hope my deodorant works. I raise a scented wrist to my nose and breathe in the lovely perfume. The queue moves slowly. Eventually a young man asks what I would like. I say, 'One of these and one of those and two lattes please?' and give my best smile and he finds the time to smile back, so I must have passed. I pay and eventually carry the tray to the table.

'There you are girlfriend. I saw you flirting with that good looking boy.' Kayleigh jokes.

'I wasn't.'

'That smile. I bet his penis is straining against the zip.'

'You're terrible. And embarrassing. But I did well didn't I? You have no idea how much courage I needed to do that.'

'I know I tease but I think the world of you Summer. By the way, do you like your new name?'

'I quite do.'

'It suits you.'

I suddenly want to cry and she sees this.

'Don't cry darling. I can imagine that giving in to your buried emotions must be a shock.'

I manage a smile. I want to bite my lip but remember I have lipstick and I shouldn't get that on my teeth. I suck in a cheek and bite on that. Slowly I recover. When she sees that I have control over my emotions she speaks again.

'I'm sorry, all this has been too quick, too much. I am so wrong. I thought you were much more comfortable in recognising the girl within than it seems you are. The last thing I want is to harm you. Shall we go home and you can be Peter again?'

I say nothing. I can't because I am so emotional I may say the wrong thing. I put a finger to my lips as a sign for her to be silent. I don't want any pressure one way or the other. Up until now, I have avoided any personal decision in my life, leaving it to others to manage me, where I live, what school I attend and even how I dress, although I have always wanted to be smart and clean, as much as my poor budget would allow.

I can see myself mirrored in a window the other side of the Mall. It's a ladies' wear shop.

'You stay here,' I command her.

I walk into the shop and look at the dresses and browse the undies, shorts, skirts and handbags. A shop girl asks if I need help and I shake my head and say I'm just browsing. She turns away and straightens some ladies' tops on the hangers.

I see a skirt I really like and it is I think, my size. I don't know whether I'm an eight or a ten. I take both and go to the changing room. It's actually the eight that fits and it's beautiful I think, red but with blue, yellow and white flowers and will look nice with a white top, the first female clothing I've bought. I pay and emerge with my bag.

I return to Kayleigh who looks worried and uncomfortable.

'What's that?' She asks.

'It's my answer.' I hand her the bag and she takes out the skirt.

'For you?'

I bite the inside of my lip and manage a nod.

'Well nice choice sister!' The woman at the next table smiles, I suppose at two girls sitting enjoying life.

'I'm glad you approve.'

She puts a hand on mine across the table. 'You're sure? We can go home now and you can revert?'

'What? And never wear my lovely new skirt?'

'Finish your coffee and cake then Summer and let's do the shops.'

We eat our cake and watch the people and some boys pass and I can't help but notice how they stare and I wonder whether they can see through my disguise.

'Those boys really stared. Do I really look OK?'

'Absolutely. You're a pretty girl, really beautiful. A different look but not boy, girl, attractive and unusual. That's why they looked, two pretty fascinating girls having coffee.' She turns and speaks to a man of about thirty at a nearby table and hands him her phone. He snaps us, faces side by side and then in profile our faces just a few inches apart and then another of us naturally at the table and I'm bringing the cup to my lips.

'Actually I think if your hair was long and straight, you would be even more stunning. Perhaps you should go chestnut, with your blue eyes and then we really would look like sisters.'

'That taxi driver!' I say. 'I wanted to die when you said we were lesbians in the sisterhood.'

'Aren't we? I am and I hope you are as my girlfriend. I'd love to kiss you right now, my little frightened rabbit, but we don't want to spoil our lippy do we.'

I say nothing except smile and this is so fun, like being under cover, in danger of discovery although apparently I'm not. I pass and I feel good. I'm keeping my slim legs together and they seem to stretch forever from the hem of my mini skirt down to the tips of my toes and it's thrillingly good.

'I think we should do shoes first. Don't worry about undies, I have lots we can share and keep your stuff in my closet then mum won't ask questions unless you want to come out?'

'No this is a one off, to please you.'

'Oh, I thought you were enjoying being a girl, being beautiful and having admiring glances and of course, buying a skirt, for yourself? So we will be wasting our time and my money looking at shoes if this is a one off, a bit of an adventure, taking a tour into girly land.' She is quite angry. 'Fuck you Peter.'

'I'm still confused, frightened. What if your parents disapprove and send me back to the home? I'd just want to die.'

Her anger turns to concern. 'Don't say that. Never say you would want to die. Mum won't send you back, honest, I know her and she won't. She already thinks you feminine though not effeminate. You are so sweet natured. You talk like a girl and you are graceful. She told me you should have been a girl and asked whether that was why I had chosen you as my companion.'

'Did you choose. Who else was in the running?'

'Well no one. But I needn't have chosen you. I knew you were right, that day we met in the Mall and we three teased you. You are so sweet, so femme. Still want to go home?'

'I'd like to look at shoes.'

'Why?'

'Just I want to know what it's like wearing heels.'

'Oh I see, just a bit of voyeurism, a foray into our world. How do you feel Summer?'

'Frightened.'

'Well that's something girls feel a lot, walking alone and a crowd of boys walk towards you and swarm around and subtly, accidentally touch you, or worse and you just hope they won't do anything. Even sitting in a cab, you hope the taxi driver is actually taking you home and not stopping in some leafy glade and trying it on. What else do you feel?'

'I feel pride in my appearance. I do feel attractive and I love my long legs in this brill skirt of yours.'

'How I wish you were a girl already. I'd have hidden your clothes and we would have been in bed all day. I would love to put my fingers in you and taste you.'

I feel faint. I'm imagining what she says happening and I want it too. If I'm honest with myself, I have never been this happy in my fourteen and some years. I have hated myself, for being a dunce at school, for being the product of a feeble mum and a thug, criminal dad and my birth the wrong side of the tracks. I had little going for me except, yes even I know, I was a nice looking boy. Mum was pretty in her young day, dad was a good looking young man in the wedding photos. Those are my best inheritances.

'That's a lovely dream Kayleigh.'

'What, having my fingers in you?'

'Hush,' I whisper, 'I'm sure that lady is listening.'

'It's not against the law to be lesbian,' she says loudly, 'come on darling, lets get out of here. People listen in to conversations between lovers.'

We leave and we run giggling down the concourse and into H&M and immediately she is into shopping mode, pulling stuff from the racks and holding it against herself and looking in the mirrors. I join in too and we move through and she gathers items as we go and then we get to the shoes and she finds my thirty-nines in a four inch stiletto and I try that on and walk about and actually it is not so hard after all. I stop in front of the mirror and look and I feel almost overwhelmed, head swimmingly overcome by my own image. These are cheap shoes but they do the same job for my legs as if they cost hundreds. I look and feel like a young colt I saw in Wales that seemed all leg.

'Do you like?'

'I do,' I say. 'My first heels.'

'Why not try these?' She holds out some almost the same but with bows on the toe and in cream that would go better with my skirt. I try them on and they so look brilliant with my outfit.

'These ones,' I say clasping them to my half fake bosom.

'I'll go and buy them now, then you can wear them, right now. Meanwhile look at the ballets and some loafers, perhaps some slippers or ballets you can wear around the house.'

She disappears leaving me with a pile of clothes we are going to try on and I look at ballets and loafers and find some I like. The ones for the house have ornamentation in the shape of swirls of coloured sequins. The other pair are sky blue. They are so pretty.

She returns and gives me the heels. 'Wear them now.'

'What now?'

'Yes, I'd like to see you wearing them. You will feel so sexy, so girl.'

So I put them on and I feel so tall so out there, so cool and so daring in heels and a lovely jungle print mini and my girly black top. I'm now five seven, and as slim as a runway model.

'Oh my God. You look super terrific,' my Sister says. 'Oh wow, with longer hair or a radical cut, you would be so stunning.' She steps away and takes more photos and tells me how to pose. See that's another thing girls know, how to pose. Boys just stand any old way. Girls have attitude, they have practised these things in the mirror. She physically adjusts me and snaps.

We go in the changing room and we try on skirts and blouses and some little summer jackets and some wide leg trousers that she says are really in at the moment.

'Oh wow, this is such a brill day Kayleigh.'

We kiss lips, gently so as not to smudge.

She pays for the things we have selected and we leave with bags full. She swings into Accessorize, and buys me bracelets and chains and some barrettes and other girl stuff she says every girl has to own. That done we wander and window shop and we go in one of the more up market large stores and try on quality stuff and I can feel the difference in the quality of the fabrics. All the time she is teaching me about stuff girls know and boys don't, names of fabrics for example and she looks at labels to find out what materials are used, and how to clean, whereas a boy would just sling it on and buy if it fitted.

We stop at a jewellery chain and she points out two silver rings rhodium plated with zirconia solitaires and we both have Identical rings and wear them on our right hands.

'Can you pierce my friend's ears?' She asks.

The girl says, 'Of course. We offer three grades of studs, gold plated, gold and gold with zirconia. Oh and we have some that would match her ring too. The others come in sterile wrapping but I could drop these in alcohol for a few minutes.

'Yes,' Kayleigh says. 'She'll have those.'

'Don't forget, I have to go to school.'

'I know that, but you can explain can't you, you are following your hero, Lewis Hamilton.'

The girl looks at us curiously. 'You are over fifteen?' She asks.

'Oh yes, but school is a bit strict.'

'Well if I do them, they can't be taken out for at least six weeks and you have to keep them clean and put on the solution twice a day and turn them and it will hurt for a while.'

'I know. I want the zirconia.' I say. It is too tempting, like an initiation. I know men have them but I still think it essentially a girl thing.

She prepares things and I am soon done. Yes they do hurt and I know I have really crossed a line into girl territory with my ring and matching studs.

We have a bowl of Singapore noodles and spicy chicken for lunch. It's really tasty food. We make use of the ladies and I'm surprised it is so much more sanitary than the boys, I mean just the smell is so much better, and it's clean in the wash basin area with a shelf to put a handbag and there's hand cream as well as soap.

'A film now?' She suggests.

'Gosh yes OK, but how are we getting home?'

'Same way we came. A taxi. How are those ears?'

'Hurting but it's bearable.'

She chooses Wonder Woman and I concur. We sit at the back in an almost empty cinema. The film starts after all the adverts and some really horrible trailers of men with axes, monsters and transformer type things obliterating humans.

We sit almost isolated and she inserts her hand between my nylon clad thighs and leaves it there. Oh my God! It is so delicious, so arousing and I turn to her and we kiss and kiss again while Wonder Woman romps through her enemies.

'Darling Summer, I love you so much. Do you like what I've done to you?'

'It's heavenly and so are you. I love you so much darling Kayleigh.' She takes my hand and places it beneath her skirt and I find she is quite wet. Taste me,' she says. I do, I lick my fingers that I extract from her panties and it's bittersweet, like I don't know, and I am possessed. I don't want this day to end. She moves her hand up under my skirt and is too close to what is there and I stop her.

'Never,' I breathe, 'I don't want you to touch me there. I know what happens and I can't control it and it is so male. If I do this, become a girl and that is what I have to do, I know that, then I don't want you to ever remember what that does or how it makes me feel. I hate it and have hated it each year more. If I could, I would cut it from me now.'

We are blessed that there is no one else near and I whisper these words and in reply she kisses me and places a hand upon my breast at the same time.

113

After we go to the ladies and then she phones for a taxi. We stand in the High Street and we see someone from school and she is coming our way just as the taxi draws in. We fall in giggling with all our packages and the taxi takes off before Deirdre Brown reaches us.

We reach home and find no parent cars, so I'm in the clear and we have an evening before us of cuddling and kissing, well I hope. I take my things up and Kayleigh comes up and rearranges her wardrobe. She places a red coat hanger one end and anything to the right of that is my stuff.

'If you decide to come out, then you can have all this in your room. I'm thinking, we ought to read about transgender, if you are serious. If not, I'll still love you but you know, well it won't be the same.'

'We can read about it on the net and see what I would have to do. It's quite frightening. I loved today because it was all new. Would it always be like that? Would you always love me?'

'Wrong questions darling. Can you live life as a boy knowing how happy you are as a girl? Can you? You have looked into a mirror and seen the future, that's how you could look. You will get proper breasts if you take drugs and you won't be all hairy. You will look more like a girl in face and body. You need to think clearly.'

"I thought you wanted me to?'

114

'Of course I love you as a girl, but this is serious now, not just a bit of fun and a kiss and cuddle in the cinema. It has to be something you desperately want. You need to look into the crystal again and see what your future would be as a man and perhaps see what life will be for you as a woman.'

'What I know is, I don't want to be like dad, nor like your dad. Nor do I want to be hairy. Even if I look at stars, like the guys who come on Graham Norton, they are like a shop window for male, I mean nicely groomed and smart, but that's not how I see me. I see myself as one of the girls on his sofa. We have been watching it and I came to think last time we watched, I don't even want to look like or behave like any of them, not even Eddie Redmayne or Johnny Depp or Orlando Bloom, even though they are pinups. I don't relate to boys. I've always admired women and wanted to be a girl.'

'So who would you like to be?'

'Keira, Keira Knightley, I think she's wonderful, or Anne Hathaway in my fave film, oh lots of lovely women. Or you.'

'Bless you. I feel a bit better about things. I didn't sleep a lot. I was so worried that I had turned you. I have been so selfish and reckless, treating you like a doll, here for my amusement. You do like being a girl, don't you? The clothes and makeup and well, me loving you as I do.'

'It's not just that. It's a more tender world. People generally treat girls in a more affectionate way, it's softer. I haven't had much softness in my life. But it's not that either, it's just everything, clothes, attitudes, the way the World sees me and I see the World. It's body dysphoria too, I hate these boy bits and it's distressing for me having them, just as much as it would be for you having some horrible growth or skin blemish.'

She kisses me. 'I never realised all that. I've opened a door and all this has spilled out. Oh of course I was telling the truth, that I could see the girl behind the façade, but I never realised you carried so much pain.' She kisses me and looks searchingly into my face. 'I'm sorry you have all this pain. I should never have played your emotions as I have, dressing you and pushing you. I've been so irresponsible and yet, perhaps I have done the right thing for the wrong reasons?'

'I'm glad you gave me the push I needed. I've longed, dreamt, pictured. I've cried and even prayed. I even thought about death because the future looked so unattractive. Let's read.'

We read up about the treatments, the T blockers and the oestrogen and progesterone. Then we researched some of the sites like on Facebook and there were all these brilliant, lovely looking girls that had been boys.

'Oh wow.' I say. 'They look so good so pretty the young ones. If I'm going to do this, then the sooner the better. I need to see my doctor and hope he will give T blockers.'

'Put his number in your phone, I'll put it in mine too. Before school Monday, we'll ring. It will give you tomorrow to really think about things. Now I guess we better go to bed.'

I take off my makeup and clean my face as she has taught me. I keep my knickers on and dress in the nightie and we are soon in bed, cuddling and kissing, her hand between my thighs but careful not to touch you know what, and my hand in her thighs, touching. I'm soon asleep and I sleep soundly.

'What the hell's going on?' The strident voice frightens me awake. I turn and find Rosalind in the doorway.

'We trusted you Peter.' She has moved into the room and stands over us.

'Mum it's not like that. She's transgender mum. Look!'

Kayleigh throws the sheet back and reveals me in the nightie that has risen up around my waist in the night and I only have these white lace panties hiding me. I pull the nightie down quickly.

'Why haven't you said?'

'Because mum, she, I call her Summer, Summer has been thinking about it, and she is phoning the doctor to start treatment tomorrow.'

Rosalind sits down on the bed. 'You're sure no sex? I know what you're like Kayleigh, so dominant.'

'Yes mum, I have pushed Summer to think about things and mum, I better own up, we went to the Mall yesterday and bought her some clothes, girl clothes mum. Look.' She springs out of bed and opens her wardrobe.

'We were going to keep it secret. All the things to the right of the red hanger are hers mum, we bought them yesterday, look the labels are still on some.'

'Why a secret?'

'Because, because she was shy and didn't want to be sent back to the home.'

The lies seemed to trip off Kayleigh's lips so easily.

'So why is Summer in your bed?'

'Why were you in Davina's mum. Oh yes we do love each other like you and Davina but mum, I don't love boys and I ignore her boy bits. I don't touch there and she hides it mum, she hates it.'

'Right. I'm too tired now. I'm going to bed, I've been up all night. You two can make lunch. There's a leg of lamb to cook in the fridge. I'll get up at twelve and then this afternoon we'll have a long chat. You better be Summer, Summer.'

'Yes mum.' I say.

She gives a look and a half smile. Perhaps I will not be returned to the home. Her smile gives hope but inside I boil and I go to the loo. My stomach has filled with gas, I suppose from fear and nerves.

I go back to the bedroom after my shower and I'm in tears of fear, not of coming out as female but of the wrath of Ros and wonder whether I will be sent back to the home.

Chapter 10.

We get up and of course I am Summer. I dress myself and do makeup and it's not a bad job I do. We breakfast and then we walk down to the local shop for mint sauce which apparently is eaten with lamb. Seems a funny thing to do but still.

I feel totally liberated in my little top and mini, my blue ballets on and my makeup and my hair that I'm going to let grow until it's right down past my shoulder blades.

We hold hands practically all the time. Some boys hanging about with a couple of scuzzy girls turn to watch us and then make stupid noises. I know we look like class against their girl companions. I'm frightened. I'm doubly vulnerable aren't I, I mean as a girl and if they found my real identity, god knows what they would do to me, to us.

The walk back was lovely, we looked at the flowers in gardens and talked to a neighbour for a bit who was obviously interested in who I was, and I was introduced as Summer, her step sister.

I don't know how she thinks these lies up so quickly. Anyway, I don't think lying matters as long as it doesn't harm anyone. Other people don't have a right to expect the truth on matters that don't concern them do they? No.

We set about cooking and bung the joint in the hot oven and set the timer for twenty minutes then we have to turn it down, Kayleigh is in command. I put on the nice femme apron and I tie it behind me in a bow, doing it myself that is something every girl knows how to do. It's not hard. I'm surprised I do it so easily.

I'm dog's body and peel potatoes and shuck fresh peas, though I read, frozen peas are just as good if not better for you and a whole lot easier. I do cauliflower and carrots as well and put some mint sauce in a little cut glass container that I'm then told is for mustard. Doesn't matter as we are not using mustard with lamb. Kayleigh teaches me to par boil the potatoes and dry them before putting them in with the meat. All is well under way when Rosalind comes down at twenty past twelve. We have made stewed plumbs too.

She enters the kitchen still looking tired and I think looking testy. 'Let me look at you Summer.'

I stand like I'm on a parade and then I relax and though I've not done it before, I do a little pirouette.

'Very pretty.' She says.

'Thank you mummy. I'm sorry it was such a shock us sharing the bed. We don't do anything except cuddle.' I say.

'I just wish you had confided in me.'

121

'Yes mum. It just sort of crept up on me. Just like Kayleigh realised how I felt and encouraged me to come out. You can understand, it's taken a lot of courage, but I so like being Summer and it makes me feel happy.'

No more is said then and we all help finish off the meal and then we sit and eat and all is pleasant again.

When lunch is over Ros says, 'So tell me about it. Why now?'

'I have only just come to the conclusion that I should do something before I become a hairy monster. No mummy that's not really it at all. I have had these thoughts in my head for years only with dad first being on the run and then in jail and with mum being in and out of hospital and then I was in the home, there was no opportunity.'

'And you have really thought about this? It's such a big step.'

'I have thought about it for years. This is a last ditch thing before the hated male puberty really kicks in and makes my life not worth living. Well hopefully, the doctor can put me on testosterone blockers until such time as they are satisfied that I'm sane and I know what I'm doing. The blockers just delay secondary sex characteristics and give breathing space.'

'So before, when you had makeup and you said Kayleigh, you were practising, was that true?'

122

'She didn't know then that I had all these thoughts in my head, and I was a bit overcome and, well embarrassed. No boy likes to admit he's like, girlie. After you told Kayleigh off, we didn't do it again, I mean makeup. I didn't want to get in trouble or get her into trouble. Yesterday, no Friday evening, I said how I felt and she called me Summer and I started sharing her bed, just for company and security because I was in turmoil and I'd confided and I was so worried that I would be returned to the home in disgrace. It's sort of all happened, because in the home, I couldn't do anything about it, it just wouldn't have worked with some of the nutters we had there. Before that, my family were dysfunctional. This seemed the right time, really the first opportunity. I have to confess that being with Kayleigh, I was so jealous of how she looked and how she dressed and how others behaved around her that it just made me feel even worse about myself.'

I think I lied almost as well as Kayleigh, but then who is completely honest? And then I think, actually what I've said is practically the truth, the essence of it is correct. Politicians, estate agents, car salesmen, just people, tell little and big fibs all the time. What I knew was that I had admitted to myself at last that little tough guy was actually a fraud. I wanted to be a girl and had always felt that way but had buried my feelings, submerged my real persona because for at least the last decade, I was not in a position to assert my real self. I mean my dad who taught me to

123

punch people in the throat, would hardly have been pleased.

I also wanted to protect my darling Kayleigh from censure by her mum and dad. It is true to say that she pushed me in this direction without knowing my predilection but in no way had she 'perverted' me from the narrow road of cisgender heterosexual life. She had aroused what was always there lying dormant.

'So this is not the fault of Kayleigh doing things that I asked her not to do? She hasn't turned you?'

'Mum!' Kayleigh says tearfully.

'Mum,' I say, 'you mustn't think that. It's just not true. Friday after you had gone to wherever, I asked if she would make my face and then when she had done, I asked if I could dress as well, and she thought it a bit of fun. I did, undies and a mini and a top and it just felt wonderful. So then I said I wished I could buy my own stuff and she said well you can't buy girl stuff looking like a boy and so we went to the Mall with me dressed as a girl and Kayleigh generously paid for my clothes. It was the best day ever and I felt real, for the first time I was the person I wanted to be. That's it.'

'When were you going to tell me?'

'I said I would make an appointment with the doctor and see what he has to say and then I would ask him to speak to you. It's such a mess.' I stopped, my voice box contracted so I couldn't carry on because my emotions have really caught up and all those years of hiding behind a façade are melted away leaving my real persona exposed, denuded of the thin skin of reputed thuggery.

Rosalind takes me in her arms and buries her face in my hair. 'Well, it's out in the open now and I can help. So Kayleigh, what have you spent?'

'I can work it out mum but it's the bare essentials she needed.'

'Yes but we get paid to look after her, so I will pay and then see what else she needs, like PJs or nighties, tights, more skirts and tops, shoes and trousers or jeans and shorts, a bathing costume, cosmetics and toiletries.'

'Oh mum, thank you. I was so upset that I had made you cross and you were cross with Kayleigh who is just the best, mum, really kind.'

'All right Summer, I get it, you two are in love. Well who am I to argue against that.'

'Does that mean we can sleep together too?'

'Yes but God help your hides if you get pregnant Kayleigh.'

'Mum, I'm lesbian.'

'Yesterday mum,' and I tell about the taxi driver.

Mum laughs and then says, 'You need to be careful. Some people really hate us lesbians or gay people or trans. Now have you both done homework?'

'Mostly mum.' I say.

'Really, with all this going on? Now here's the bargain. Do your homework and more this afternoon. Thursday, late night shopping we go to Westgrove and we buy you more things, some dresses too. If this is going on, then at sometime we will have to tell school and you will have to brave being out.'

'I know mum. Bang goes my street cred. I'll be a target for every bully in the school.'

'Maybe not, if you tell everyone you are going to live with an aunt somewhere away and then you go back as a girl, with a different name and saying that Peter was a cousin. If you can pull it off.'

'I don't know whether it would work. They are sure to recognise me.'

'Perhaps if you had spectacles?'

'We can try. They have them in H&M, just plain glass. There is still my voice. Sometimes it's OK, sometimes I slip. That's the most difficult thing.'

'Then we find someone who can help, a voice therapist. You look well, I mean you would pass as a girl. Summer, is that really what I'm to call you?'

I nod shyly.

'Summer, you really have to think this through. I'm not yet convinced that this is not just a sudden impulse, the result of a vulnerable boy mixing with a brash and dominant girl.'

'I have, don't you think I have? Night after night, no actually day in day out, minute after minute. As we find more information, I will think it through but really Kayleigh has just awakened what has always been there.'

'You still have to think hard about it. I want you to come home each day and become Summer. Perhaps you will tire of it.'

'No mum I won't. It's real mum.'

'Very well. Off you both go and work hard.'

We go upstairs and work in Kayleigh's room and she tests me on Geography and then helps again with Maths.

'Thanks for defending me. You were terrific.' She says.

'Well I love you and I'm wearing your knickers so I can't but, can I? Kiss.'

We kiss and giggle and we now have permission to sleep together. I say, 'Are we still sleeping in your bed?'

'You betcha darling Summer, my sexy sister.'

I think life could not be better. Later as we go to bed, she removes my makeup, making sure it's all removed so no one will notice at school.

In the morning it's back into boy mode and I hate it. I go down and I think to phone my doctor, the one I had in the home.

'Don't phone your doctor. I have registered you with our surgery. I will book an appointment and go with you. Do you want to go there as a boy or a girl?'

'Of course a girl.'

'Then I'll arrange it for about five so you can come home and change. She will ask lot's of questions, so be prepared and speak up for what you want. I shall speak to her first so she's prepared.'

'Thanks mum.' I kiss her cheek. We go to school and it's really horrid being Pete again and so people don't notice, Kayleigh and I keep it all casual, like brother and sister rather than lovers. It sort of hurts when she dismisses me with a, 'See you when mum collects us.' She walks away with her mates, Sally and Janey who both show me more affection than Kayleigh. I know this is all a smokescreen but I feel so deprived and alone.

Mid morning break. I'm leaning on the red brick wall watching the boys play football. Martin looks up and sees me and boots the ball as hard as possible towards me. It hits the wall two feet from my head and bounces back into the game. I saw it come and yet didn't move, didn't flinch. That was what Martin wanted. Why he hates me, I don't know.

My phone burbles and I get a text from Mum. I find Kayleigh and show her. 'Doctor 5.10 this afternoon'. We walk away from her gang.

'Oh. Are you nervous?'

'Not yet shitless but I may be when I get there. Are you going to do my makeup?'

'As it's a special occasion yes I will. What will you wear?'

'What I wore to the Mall is in the wash. That new pink mini and the V neck shirt that is quite girly or the dark blue lace blouse. What do you think?'

'I think the pink and lace blouse would be excellent. You must be so excited?'

'Feel my hand.'

'Oh its so cold.'

"I'm dead scared Kayleigh. What if this doctor says no?'

'Oh she won't, mum can be very forceful, like me.'

'Why were you interested in me before, you know that day in the Mall?'

'There was always something, some indefinably female feel about you. I've always thought you beautiful, even though you were a boy. Do you get that from your mum?'

'She was ever so pretty and dad was a good looking boy as a young man. He's been knocked about a bit since.'

'Well till this afternoon. I'm coming with you.'

'I just want to change now, even if these try to bully. I want to wear your little pleated skirt and blouse. Now I've made the decision, it's really hard to wait.'

'You just have to be patient. Really Summ. See what mum comes up with.'

Chapter 11.

Mum picks us up and we go home so I can change. Kayleigh actually makes me do makeup, watches as I make my face but says I have to do it myself though she had promised to do it. Well I have to learn and I like doing it. It makes me smile, seeing my face change and liking what I see as boy face that I know so well disappears and this young lady appears. I panic that I am taking too long.

I needn't have worried about being late for we arrive five minutes ahead of time and are called twenty minutes after the appointed time.

Mum and I go to the doctor leaving Kayleigh reading OK mag. When I go in I find that Dr Letitia Seymour is a pleasant looking thirty something.

'You are officially Peter Wallace but calling yourself Summer?

'Yes doctor,' I can hardly breathe the words I am so emotional and shy.

'I need to hear you Summer. I'm not hear to judge you but to listen and help. So just to put you at ease, I have had one transgender patient before, so I do know a little about it. Now big breath and tell me when you first felt like this. I have left you to last so I have the time for a long story. Leave nothing out.'

131

So I tell about my childhood, the fights between dad and mum and his violence and mum's eventual descent into prescription drug dependency. I tell about the home and some of the highly disturbed children there and how I have had to bury everything and become a loner, so no one would discern the true me.

Then I tell about Kayleigh making me up and how that put a torch to the tinder of my inner turmoil. I say that three weeks later, I ask her to do it again and how I ask to also cross dress and go to the Mall and buy my own girl stuff. How we sleep together but just cuddle.

'And you have been to school today as a boy?'

'Yes. I asked mum to take me home so I could change and do makeup before coming here.'

'Why?'

'Because I wanted you to see the real me, not a sulky silent school boy, which is what I was.'

'But as a girl, you are not sulky?'

'No I'm full of joy, though I'm a bit frightened of discovery, that someone will see that I'm really a boy in a skirt.'

'I don't see why they would. You look like a lovely teenage girl. Your features are not particularly boy, in fact a rather attractive unusual girl, not in the slightest like a boy. Do you feel confident?'

'I'm becoming so, it's not easy, easier for a girl to pass as a boy than the other way. My voice is my main worry.'

'Well first I have to see that you really are a boy, so behind the screen and on the couch, you needn't take your shoes off, oh you have. Up you get and panties down and knees up, and apart……….. Well, sure enough, you are a biological male. When you are dressed come back and sit.'

I return, trying to compose myself again. I'm so embarrassed.

'You found that hard didn't you?'

'Yes. It's an embarrassment.'

'Your voice does change from one register to another. Some girls, women do have quite a low register but boys talk from their belly and girls from the mouth. I will send you to a speech therapist, a lady who is very good. What else can I do?'

'T blockers. I haven't facial hair but it can't be far away and testosterone will ruin my looks.'

'Yes, well I am prepared for that. So I will give an injection and you have one a month, something to look forward to isn't it. I'll prepare the syringe. Do you want to go behind the screen or just show me a buttock?'

'I'll just show a buttock.'

I reach down with my left and pull my skirt and with the other hand lower my panties. I suppose I will have to get used to this.

She stabs me in the backside and it feels quite a large injection.

'Every month from now on, so make your appointment today. I will refer you to a clinic but the waiting list is now very long. If you can afford private medicine, then I would advise going that way. Do you have any questions?'

'I don't think so, thank you. You've been nice.'

'I have one. Are there side effects to the T blocker?' Mum asks.

'Spironolactone we consider a safe drug but no drug is entirely safe. Some people experience no problems others may get headaches or dizziness, almost certainly loss of muscle power, because your muscles will be becoming girl muscles. Your breasts may hurt and swell a little.'

I interrupt. 'They are already swollen.'

'Oh then I will have to take a look. Can you remove your top?' I pull it up around my neck and this reveals my bra and the hankies stuffed in the cups. I want to die of shame.

She feels my breasts, gently. 'Mmm,' she says, 'they are quite swollen. I suspect with the spironolactone, they'll swell more as any antigens that destroy secondary sex characteristics that make a girl a girl, are suppressed. You may get significant breast development even without oestrogen. How would you feel about that?'

'Wonderful. I really can't wait.'

She smiles. 'Well that is the answer I would expect from a transsexual. You are very convincing. This treatment is all reversible if you want to change back. Even when we start you on oestrogen, it is not the road of no return. In the long run, that will make you sterile but that is the ultimate effect of medication and surgery if you go for that. Not all do.'

'Oh I would want surgery, otherwise, I'd feel like I was acting, like a pantomime dame[5].

'Well at least we are stopping the dreaded testosterone from making you a hairy monster as you put it.

---

[5] In the UK we have a Christmas tradition of pantomime, to stories like Cinderella, Sleeping Beauty, Snowwhite in which some parts, usually the comic ones, cross dress. The prince or other lead male may also be played by a girl.

A month from now. Same day each month and I will use your buttocks as a pin cushion. Take care Summer.'

We let ourselves out of the consulting room and find Kayleigh. I make an appointment while mum and she talk. I kiss her and hold her hand as we walk to the car.

'Did you get your blocker?' She asks.

'Right in my bum. I get another in a month. I'm so relieved, I would hate that I get facial and other hair and hard muscles. It's all so yucky and being with you has emphasized the difference. I'm never going to have all your femininity and I have missed fourteen years of growing up as a little girl, but I will accept and rejoice in what I can get.'

They say nothing except Kayleigh squeezes my hand. We enter the car and settle in, fastening belts and Rosalind, mum puts the car in gear and off we go. Ros says nothing on the short journey home. In the hallway, we collect our bags of books and take them upstairs and then head into down to the kitchen for a drink.

We sit at the table with our mugs and I sip and cuddle my mug with both hands.

'So Summer was that all satisfactory?' Mum asks.

'It would have been unreasonable to ask for more than that. She was very nice and understanding and I didn't feel like I was some weird creature. I wish I could see a specialist now, but she said it could be eighteen months and I really want to take oestrogen.'

'Well she is sending me a few addresses of private consultants. The numbers of trans has increased so over the last few years, that the National Health Service is just swamped with patients, going both ways. I did a lot of research today while you were in school and I was just amazed. So Summer, be patient, we will get some contact names and we can also do some research ourselves. I am not going to let you wait all that time to see a consultant who will probably rubber stamp what Doctor Letitia says.'

'Thank you.'

'I want to get you through this and the money for a private consultation is neither here nor there. The council are I think, paying us generously to have you with us, so money is not a problem at least until it comes to the cost of surgery. That could be thirteen thousand in England, less abroad. We have time to think about it but the National Health could take years.'

'Oh mum, it just seems an impossible hill to climb.'

'No, we must think positively. First we need to find you a private consultant while keeping your name on the NHS list. Hopefully they will prescribe oestrogen if they find whatever they look for. We'll wait and see what Letitia comes up with.'

'Why not crowd fund it? If we got half the money?' Kayleigh asks.

'No. That's for people who really have nothing.' Mum says, 'Look we are paid a lot of money to keep you darling Summer. We will pay for your surgery when the time comes.'

'Oh mum, thanks. Mum you have been so great mum.' I fling myself at her and hug her and she hugs me and kisses my forehead and it's the happiest moment. I have tears of gratitude. I dab my eyes with a tissue.

'Summer it is not an easy path and if you remain convinced and I think you perhaps will, I will see you through this, so that before Uni you will be the person you want to be.'

'We could all have a holiday in Thailand, all the girls mum, Davina too?'

'Well that is an idea. What do you think Kayleigh?'

'Mum it would be nice to meet Davina. I'm sure dad would like to go somewhere with whoever he is shacked up with.'

'Samantha.'

'Samantha? Have you met her mum?'

'Yes Kayleigh. She's very nice.'

'Mum! Didn't you give her a poke in the eye?'

'No not at all. Look I married dad and then found I didn't much like men, or sex with a man and I like women. Sam has done me a favour. He gets what he wants, I get what I want. When you go to Uni, we will probably separate for good. We stay for you and it works, especially with this one here.' She reaches out and ruffles my hair.

'Thanks mum. It's good to be wanted. I was so worried that you would see me as a burden, especially with all this going on, something you never expected when I first came here.'

'There is something else we need to think about. You might want to have children with whoever is your partner. We need to bank your sperm Summer.'

'Mum?' I say embarrassed, because for one I don't want to think where and how I would provide it and that she can even speak the word that is so full of meaning in sex and defines me as male.

'It's no good burying your head and pretending, we have to think of the realities. If you two stayed together, would you want babies Kayleigh?'

'Don't know mum. At the moment anything like that is a long way away from my thoughts. But, just in case, it wouldn't hurt would it? I mean if I had babies and we are together, then It would be nice if they are really yours Summer wouldn't it?'

'Yes, I just think it's yucky. I hate even touching myself down there.'

'Golly, you disguised your girliness well. I didn't realise it was as bad as that. That must just be awful. No wonder you won't let me see you nude.'

'Now you know, I'm severely weird.' I say.

'But loveable.' Kayleigh says.

'I don't know what Harry will say. Oh well, we can't help that can we.'

When Thursday arrives we don't go to the Mall because we have a lot of homework and mum says, that comes before anything.

The week has flown by. Friday afternoon arrives. We are picked up from school and told to be good and to be careful. We promise and we intend to be good, we don't get up to mischief. Mum has left supper for us a salad with ham and cold beef. When she has finished her instructions, she is off to see Davina open in a new play and of course we shall not see her until Sunday morning. I change into my girl clothes, an everyday occurrence after school and I have pocket money to spend so tomorrow after processing Kayleigh's orders, now my daily task, we plan on another raid in the Mall but this time our local one. It's bigger than Westgrove, that's the attraction.

We fancy chips so we walk the quarter mile to the local chippy and bring back one bag to share between us with the salad.

After that we do homework. Brainbox still helps me and she is so brilliant. Now I'm happy, I find I can grasp stuff and retain it.

Of course we sleep together and I'm gloriously happy. All the time I'm learning girl stuff, she teaches me even when I think I know, but I don't resent it. There is so much that girls are taught by their mums that boys never know, things like periods that even though I will never have one, I need to know because girls are expected to have the knowledge but also the names of different materials and colours, sizes and bra fitting, different styles of panties and all the different varieties of clothing girls have that boys don't, like dropped back or bare shoulder, slashed. I never realised that boys and girls were so different.

These are not the only things. On the whole girls are more tolerant and sweeter natured but they can also be cruel and they have tongues that probably bite more than boys. Girls operate on emotions and they are interested in other people's emotions, boys hardly ever talk about how they feel. It's all about sport and lascivious comments about girls. Well that's what I think so far. I like the girl world.

Morning comes and I do my own makeup. I check my bag that I have everything and we walk to the bus stop. This is even more of an adventure than last week because we are going local and there may be kids from school in the Mall. I just hope that my cover is not blown or life at school will be hell. Little tough guy will be gone forever.

We walk the Mall and we go into all the cheap shops just looking but taking notes because I want some really nice trousers and I fancy a couple of blouses. Nothing jumps out at me, though I see a knitted top that's really sweet but which Kayleigh says will fall to bits and snag like mad because it's such an open weave.

We walk on and I'm sure I see that creep who I thought followed me before. I don't think he recognises me in my girl guise, I hope not. I'm on the second floor walking towards the escalators when he comes up and he doesn't even look my way. Brilliant. Perhaps he never was watching me in particular or he might be a Mall detective, I know they have them. He looks sort of familiar, like someone I used to know.

I take a passage that leads to New Look that is outside the Mall in a side road where Kayleigh is supposed to meet me because we want to look at their shoes. I fancy some more heels and she will advise as usual.

I'm swinging along my bag banging against my belly. I feel great and I hum to myself Symphony, Clean Bandit and Zara Larsen, my fave of the moment and she's my idol. I'm imagining I'm her.

The hand that clamps across my face smells of things I don't like, nicotine and man and the skin is rough. He has me so tight my neck hurts. I try to kick out but I can't breathe, his hand covers both mouth and nose. The barrette drops from my hair and I want to stop for it but I am forced along, my arms pinned back by his other arm and then two more hands seize me and I'm thrown in the back of this van and the door bangs shut and is locked. I'm terribly frightened and imagine it is like that film Room and I'll be kept in some shed and when they find I'm not a girl, they will probably rape me anyway or just kill me there and then.

They drive and drive and I roll about in the back as they go round corners. There is just nothing to hang onto and I can't see out. There's a box containing something and I use that to wedge myself against the side. That is better than rolling around and getting bruised. It's pretty dark in here, just a crack of light around one of the two doors where it's a bad fit.

I take my girl shoes off and I try kicking at the doors but they don't give at all and I just hurt a foot. I want to cry but that won't help either.

I'm frightened. I want a pee and we keep driving for what seems hours. The roads were noisy with other traffic but now I only hear the rumble of our engine and the tyres of this rough old van. I think I have cut my hand and I don't want to get blood on my clothes. At last we stop.

I bang on the side of the van. I don't know what for because I'm sure there is no escape until they have done what they want with me. I'm terribly fearful of what that may be.

Chapter 12.

The van door opens and I don't hesitate to exit. I know they will get me anyway. My wrist is gripped in a horny hand with all the strength I imagine a crocodiles jaws possess.

'Ow,' I scream as girlie as I can, 'You're hurting me.'

'No good screaming, we're in the middle of nowhere Peter.'

How do they know my boy name? I can't bother with that now. I need to pee really urgently.

'I need to pee,' I say.

'Well go on then, we're not stopping you.'

'Don't watch.'

'God almighty, what would your fucking father say if he could see you now.'

The other man says, 'Get up against the barbed wire fence and do what you gotta. We ain't got no toilet paper.' I squat near the fence and watch them and one by one they turn their backs. Well that's something. I think I recognise the voice of number two. He sounds like dad so I wonder whether he's my uncle Carl. I use a paper hankie to wipe and try to bury it under a clump of grass while pulling up my panties. I'm seized again.

145

'Right Peter, remember me?'

'My scumbag uncle Carl, I'm guessing.'

'Don't she talk posh an' all?'

'What do you want?' I'm relieved that it seems they won't kill me. They know who I am so they have captured me for a reason.

'If you're going to be sensible, you can sit up front, but no funny stuff.'

So there I am stuck between these two hairy oafs on the bench, legs astride the hump in the middle where the gear stuff is. 'What do you want? We haven't any money.'

'No but your dad has.'

'He's in prison.'

'Yeah we know and I just got out.'

The van rumbles through what seems to be endless hills. We pass a few isolated farms, stonewalls fields of cows and sheep and woodland. It's dusk already and then full dark and we stop by what appears to be a lonely barn in the middle of nowhere. We climb out and the big ape who I guess was my captor, holds my wrist so there's no escape.

I lose my shoe as I climb down and I shout, 'My shoe you great ape.' And I bend and scrabble for it, find it with my fingers and slip it on my foot. We walk the few yards to this old barn. It's absolutely pitch inside but they light a lantern, so they must have prepared things in advance.

'What do you want?'

''Ain't you the young lady now Peter. So what the hell's going on with my nephew? Why are you all got up like a girl? We been watching you on and off for weeks.'

'Yes I saw you in the Mall. I thought it was a pervert chasing me.'

'Alright, that'll do. Be civil to your Uncle. So what's going on?'

'I'm trans.'

'What a trannie?'

'No not a fucking trannie. Transgender, or rather transsexual.'

'You mean they're going to lop off your dickie dangler?'

'If that's how you want to put it yes.'

'Christ! What brought that on?' The big bastard asks.

'I didn't want to grow up to be an ugly sod like you?'

'Cheeky little fucker aren't you?' Says the Ape.

'Why have you brought me here?'

'We're looking for your dad's hoard see. Just after we done that bank job and he clobbered the guard, you took a holiday down here and he told me he hid it in the garden while you and mum was buildin' sand castles, because then you were just a little kid and a boy. We're hopin' you can tell us were you stayed, a cottage on the coast it was, so you better remember.'

'And then what? You dig it up and dad still rots in prison and you two idiots piss off to live in Northern Cyprus or Spain and live happily ever after. Which one of you two goons is the girl in this partnership? I'm guessing it's you uncle Carl as you're the smaller one.'

'Well I'll say that, you got your dad's lip and your mum's wit. Look what happened to her and that's how you'll end up if I have any more of it. I'll beat you silly.'

'So what if I can't remember the cottage?'

'Then we'll tie you up somewhere and we'll be long gone.'

'When dad hears he will blooming kill you, not for me but for the money. I hope he catches up.'

'You better find it Peter.'

'Summer, my name is Summer.'

'Christ. What the fuck's a name matter?'

'Because that's who I am now.'

'Well you better get your beauty sleep. We'll have to tie you hand and foot. Don't try and run off because we'll do you over you if we have to.'

'Haven't you brain boxes brought any food? Surely you thought of that.'

'Yeah we got sandwiches and water and beer. I'll get 'em.' The big oaf says.

He goes out and I hear the van door sort of crunch as it opens on worn out hinges. I look at Carl and he is watching me.

'What?' I ask, my nose in the air.

'You've turned into quite a hoighty toighty little bitch haven't you *Summer?* Fuck, I never thought my brother's son would turn out queer.'

'I don't expect your mother expected you to turn out to be a shiftless thug either.'

'You better watch your tongue because big Jim will snap and I'll have as much chance of pulling him off you as I would a bull mastiff.'

'Well I figured he had a dogs brain to go with his breath.'

'Don't say I didn't warn you.'

'He's gone a long time.'

'Probably shaking hands with the wife's best friend.'

'What?'

'Having a pee.'

'Oh that was vulgar!'

'Oh your bloody ladyship! Come off it, you're your dad's child.'

'Yes unfortunately. I never wanted to be like him and I've escaped, at least I had until your pet gorilla grabbed me. I hope dad rots in prison for what he did to mum.'

The Gorilla enters with flasks and a carrier bag.

'What no picnic hamper, strawberries and champers?' I ask sarcastically. 'I hope those sandwiches aren't made by your own sweet hands Mr Gorilla, because if they are, count me out. I wouldn't like to think where they have been, picking your arse I wouldn't wonder.'

'Fucking lippy little cow you have turned into. I bounced you on my knee when you was a nipper. You sat there a gigglin'.'

'I know better now and know an idiot when I see one.'

He answered with a punch to my gut that felled me. He stood over me like a tower block and I thought a boot was coming in. I curled up like a hedgehog.

'That's enough out of both of you. Lay off Jim, and you, keep that yap shut girl.'

'You want to keep that on a chain.' I gasp.

'And you want to know when to shut your mouth. He could kill you with one punch. Sit down on that straw bale and get your breath, then have a drink and a sandwich, bought from a supermarket, so if they make you ill, sue them. Here, BLT or cheese and ham?'

I wipe the tears from my eyes and a sob escapes.

'Not as strong as you thought. Let that be a lesson Peter.'

'It's Summer. I shan't cooperate unless you get that right and if you touch me again, you can just go play with yourselves.'

'OK Summer. Christ. Just be a nice girl for us and we'll be nice to you.' Carl says a little more kindly.

I make no reply. I'm still hurting from rolling about in that van and the punch and feeling a bit sick too, but I must eat. I haven't eaten all day. I still have my bag and I haven't touched it and nor have they thought to search it. I mean it's so tiny, holds a small purse, my cash card that mum Ros signed me up for and a lippy, mascara, eyebrow pencil and my phone. They haven't thought to take that off me. They really are a couple of dimwits. Still so am I or I would have connected with google and put tracking on. Shit. Should have done that when I was in the back of that van, rolling about like a log in a wild river.

They have to sleep sometime so I hope I have the opportunity. The trouble is I am also damned tired. I feel beaten and dishevelled.

I take a drink of tea from the flask cap. The gorilla is drinking straight from the flask. Typical.

I have recovered enough to chew on a sandwich and it's OK, from Marks and Spencer I see, so no expense spared. I try to ignore them. I sit apart and have pushed my bag behind me, out of sight and I hope therefore out of their minds.

I finish the sandwich and eat the second and ask Uncle for some more tea. He gives me half a cup. I drink that and I say to Carl, 'I'm really tired. I need to pee again, then can I go to sleep?'

'Yeah kid. See it's better to behave like a young lady and be nice. All that lip don't do you no good.'

He takes me to the rear of the barn and then turns his back. I squat again and pee a red-hot stream into the straw strewn earth floor. I find another tissue from my bag and wipe and pull up my panties. I stand and do what I can with my skirt and blouse to look a bit clean and shipshape.

I turn and find Uncle watching me. 'You are a girl.' He says. 'I have to tie you. Hands in front or behind?'

'In front Uncle Carl. You're not going to kill me are you?'

'Bless you no. Is that why you have been so stroppy?'

'Well you haven't exactly played the doting uncle have you, and your pet gorilla, where did you find it.'

'He was also a family friend and he really did bounce you on his knee.'

'I don't remember. Just tie my hands and let me sleep Uncle Carl.'

He studies me as if trying to see whether I'm up to tricks. I try to look as pathetic and as hopeless as I feel. I'm absolutely whacked, physically and mentally. I just want to curl up and cry. I want to feel the arms of Ros around me or feel the soft flesh of Kayleigh against my nightie. I want a shower and to sit in it for a long time. I want to wash my hair and scrub my body. I want to cry, blub, let tears flow in rivers down my cheeks in self-pity but I won't. I will appear beaten as I almost am. I will appear like a mound of ashes and yet within lurks a heat that when stirred will burst aflame again and when I can, I will revenge myself on these two. I don't care about dad's stash they can have that, but their treatment of me will if I can find a way, be revenged.

He ties my hands each separately and with enough slack so my blood will still flow and yet my hand is captured and then he ties my two hands together. He spreads clean straw for me and I lie upon it. He throws his jacket across my legs. I'm asleep in minutes and I sleep like the dead even trussed as I am.

I awake to bird song. It must be really early for the dawn chorus is in full song but the light is still cold grey. They, when I look, are still asleep. I find a string fastens me from my wrists to uncle's leg, so no scape is possible. I will just after yesterday's acts of bravado, stay stumm. Somehow I have to outwit these halfwits that dad has cheated apparently of the proceeds of the bank job. Then another thought comes to me. Maybe I can get a share, enough to pay for surgery and then I think that is immoral. It's not my money. It came from a bank and although we all think banks are amorphous organisations that have cheated us over the length of the Blair Government at least, they are essential and their money is actually our money. Besides which, that poor guard was hurt and dad is still rightly in prison for the injury he did.

Better I think, would be to get a reward not only for returning the money, but for the capture of Carl and the Gorilla. I have to lay a false trail somehow, so they don't think I have a phone in my bag. If I ask to make a call, using their phones or a call box if we find one that still works, maybe they will believe that I have no phone. I will say Ros took it away because I kept playing games on it at meal times. Why not? I'd believe that.

I lie and try to think things out. I feel sure that Uncle Carl won't kill me but the Gorilla, he may be another matter. He may have dangled me on his knee when I was a baby but that is far from being kind to me now. If it's him or me and money is involved I have no chance. They are still snoring. The Gorilla is worst of all and he seems to half wake every tenth snore, then snorts and starts all over again. Time passes very slowly.

Chapter 13.

I must have fallen asleep again because I look at my watch and find it's after six o'clock. I lie and see pigeons roosting on the rafters and hope they will not shit on me. I give a jerk on the cord that connects me to Carl and he wakes. I want him to so he can untie me. For one thing I want to pee and I want to check my make up. I must look an absolute fright.

Sunlight filters through the wooden walls and I can smell the straw and the slight musky scent of animals that probably sheltered in this place in the past. It has no romance for me, unlike the scene I remember in a James Bond film where he spent the night with a girl in a barn in Switzerland.

'Uncle Carl!' I say. 'Untie me please. I need to pee.' I give him a kick on the foot and he sort of jerks round awake.

'What?'

'I need to pee Uncle.'

'Christ you're always wanting.'

He climbs to his feet and he struggles to untie my bindings with fat fingers with nails chewed down to the quick. Eventually I'm free. I rub my wrists.

'Thanks Uncle. I want to pee.'

'Go to the back then, where you went last night.' He says testily as though exasperated.

I go to the back and squat in what used to be an animal stall for a little privacy and I do what I need to do.

'Uncle, I haven't got a mobile, mum took it away because I played games on it. Can I borrow yours, just to say I'm OK? They'll be worried.' I start to cry, half put on but half is real concern for Ros and Kayleigh, and the distress I feel for myself.

'The police'll trace the call. Sorry kid. They'll just have to worry. We get there this morning and you find this old coastguard cottage where you stayed and we search for the box. It's metal so we shouldn't have a problem. You could be home tomorrow.'

I still snivel. It seems he has swallowed my having no mobile. He goes to the back and relieves himself then he gives the Gorilla a kick and the great oaf stirs like an ox with a horse fly bite. These guys aren't brains of Britain or they would have searched my bag.

'Wharrup,' he grunts.

'Get up, we need to get breakfast.'

The Gorilla comes to his feet. He looks even more gross in the light of day. I want to get fresh air and make for the battered door. Carl follows. He pushes me up into the van and follows, sitting himself behind the wheel. He pulls out a coverall, paint smeared navy blue.

'Get that on. They'll have a description of you and no fucking argument.'

'Then I need to take my skirt off, but I'm not doing that in front of you.'

'Christ. You are worse than a fucking girl.'

He hauls me out so I almost fall and he drags me by the hand to the rear, unlocks and thrusts me inside.

'Change in there and hurry up.'

I change into the overall. It smells and I hate it. I've got used to wearing a skirt and I like the freedom and having legs. I try not to think about who has worn this thing before. It's two sizes too large. I roll the legs up.

Carrying my bag and skirt, he helps me out of the van and escorts me to the front. He thrusts me in to sit next to the Gorilla. The Gorilla really stinks like an animal. He is so repulsive.

'I need to wash.'

'Here we go again,' Carl says. 'I want, I want. God you really are a fucking girl. Can't wait till your dad finds out about you. He'll break out of the slammer to take you in hand.'

'Yes but first he will probably kill you two idiots for stealing his stash. He's murderous when roused. I wouldn't want to be in your shoes for a million. He will track you down.'

An elbow in the ribs from the Gorilla takes my breath and my eyes water. We lurch out of the barn area and onto the road. I'm thinking about their planning. They obviously did some, because they had planned that stop at the barn. We drive through countryside with scattered farms among hills on an almost deserted road. The day that had promised much at dawn was in contrast now overcast and grey. In the distance, as we head downwards, I see rain falling and in the far distance the sea that merges into sky.

We turn onto a main road and I think run southwards. We pull into a Roadhouse. We enter, me sandwiched between the two.

The Gorilla says gruffly, 'No funny business queer boy, or I'll take your fucking head off your fucking scrawny neck.'

'I want to wash.' I say.

'Let her wash. Just check she can't get out the window, then leave her to it.'

'You sure?'

'Yeah, come on she is my niece.'

'Niece? You go for this transfuckinnonsense?'

'If it makes her happy.'

'Don't worry Mr Gorilla, I don't fancy you.'

I manage to avoid most of the blow to my kidneys. I stagger out of line and he hauls me back. We enter the place and wait to be seated. We must look an odd threesome but the girl must be used to it. She smiles and leads us to a table by the window.

The Gorilla takes my upper arm in a vice grip and we head for the loo. He thrusts me before him and we burst though the door. The three cubicles are empty. He looks at the window that is open but too narrow for a body to wriggle through, presumably to prevent people escaping without paying.

'You can leave me now Claude,' I say as though he's my butler and to my joy he does.

'No funny business. I'll be outside.'

I select a cubicle and do what I need to do. I take my lipstick and write on the wall inside the cubicle, "Help. Kidnapped. Summer Wallace. Please phone 999.' I also give Ros's number and the van number too.

160

I switch my phone on and there are a hundred missed calls. I send a message to Kayleigh, 'kidnapped by Uncle Carl, somewhere in Wales'. I put it on silent and turn the vibrate off. I place it at the bottom of my bag. I do my best to wash my face with the hand soap and toilet tissue for a flannel. I dry and do brows, mascara and lipstick, all I have. I look very pale. My skin even without foundation is luminous. I wish I had more makeup with me.

'Thanks I say,' as I exit and find a woman waiting who has been barred from entry by my minder.

'I'm sorry about my minder,' I say, 'he should have let you in, shouldn't you Mr G. Remember next time.'

'Yes miss,' he says, catching in on the act. The last thing I want is for her to see my notice and run out screaming and yelling. Anything might happen and these two might harm me to escape capture, especially Mr G.

Carl has ordered the all day breakfast for us all with extra chips. I am stuck against the window, wedged in by the man mountain. I'm as hungry as a starving wolf but without the capacity of my captors. I eat the eggs, bacon and sausage plus the mushroom but leave the hash browns but I do dig into the chips. The Gorilla takes my hash browns. He's welcome.

Carl pays and the Gorilla hauls me out of the seat and we walk to the door. A few people have been to the loo but no one has raised the alarm. Well who in their right mind reads messages. I should have written on the mirror but I was frightened Mr G would come in and check. Perhaps a message on loo paper would have worked. It's no good speculating. We are in the van and on the move, south parallel to the coast and I recognise a few names from six years ago when I was here with mum and dad. We enter the village of Cwm, I remember it because at the time we guessed how to pronounce it. After that we leave Cardiganshire and enter Pembrokeshire and pass through Fishguard and roll on down to St David's. We end up at this one horse quite attractive little settlement north of the smallest City of the UK, St David's. It has a Cathedral and under two thousand people I remember.

I see a sign for Abercastle and I shout, 'That way!' before I have even thought about it. I'm excited that those memories are returning, those mainly happy days for me, of building sandcastles, trying to body-board, eating soggy tomato and ham sandwiches, ripe Williams pears that were just sweet liquid in the mouth and bags of crisps. I remember fishing in pools, finding sea anemones, and tiny crabs that even so could nip and even tinier fish. I remember slipping on the slimy seaweed and hurting my bum and elbow. I remember finding a baby seal, a fat little off white and brown creature with big eyes looking so cuddlesome but which swore at me and bared it's teeth. The memories of being a single child, the loneliness, the despair of not being who I should be. The little treats. I cry.

'Oh for fucks sake,' says Carl irritably.

'I was remembering, everything from back then and that holiday. I can't help it. I have emotions, you two only have one, greed.'

'Belt up. Which fucking way if you remember everything?'

'Turn right and drive till we come to the farm cottages and the little shop, then we go right up the lane.'

'You sure?' asks the Gorilla.

'Yes I'm sure you moron.'

'You keep on I'll take my belt to your queer little arse.' The Gorilla says.

We reach the farm cottages, still all as neat as I remember. We turn right, up the lane that is wide enough for just one car and covered in cow muck from the passage of cows to and from the dairy and the cliff top grazing.

'Here it is, this one, that's the cottage. Just three rooms and a lavatory at the bottom of the garden.'

We pull into the parking area. There's no other vehicle so presumably it is unoccupied at the moment. It's a single story building, built of great flints from the beach, with a slate roof. The walls are all white painted and it has a central chimney.

It looks unoccupied and neglected. I suppose it is now too primitive for holidaymakers.

The two halfwits are out in a second and open the rear doors and pull out the large cardboard carton. I had wondered what it was. I can now see a metal detector.

The two brain boxes had come prepared to search for buried treasure at least. Carl looks at the cottage and knocks the door in case there is someone within. He peers in the window. Reassured that there is no one home, he kicks the door in.

'What did you do that for,' I ask, outraged.

'He may have left it in the loft or something, need to search that first. Do you remember if he did any digging or anything.'

'I remember a little mouse used to come out at night from a hole by the door and I remember it died, got caught in the door jamb.'

'Fucking hell, was that what I asked? Did he do any gardening?'

'Don't remember. Mum and I went to the beach mostly. Dad sometimes but sometimes he didn't feel like it.'

'That's probably when he was hiding it. Do you remember him having a box, one perhaps that stayed in the car?'

'It's like Treasure Island.' I say.

'Yeah and you know what those pirates done in them days, they used to bury some one with the treasure an' right now I'm lookin' at you kid.' The Gorilla says, his face full of malice.

'You wouldn't,' I say in an act of mock terror.

'Shut up the pair of you,' says Uncle Carl. 'Right there's a loft hatch. So you are going up there since you are small Summer.'

'It will be filthy and there may be rats.'

'Well too bad. Put her up there.'

The Gorilla grasps me by leg and buttock and I'm propelled upwards my head hitting the hatch cover and I'm in the dark. 'I can't see,' I say pushing the cover away. I have to scrabble all the way in and it stinks of wood smoke and mustiness and dust. I feel around and try to keep on the rafters to avoid putting a foot through the ceiling. He passes me a torch. I look around, behind a galvanised water tank and into the corners. There's insulation but only to the depth of the rafters and I'm not going to pull all that fibre glass about. I'm already coughing.

'There's nothing up here.'

'You're sure?'

'Yes I'm sure.' I cough again. 'Get me down.'

The Gorilla puts a hand up to support my foot. I tread on it and then lower the other foot onto his head. He doesn't seem that bothered. He seizes a leg and lowers me to the ground. I make for the door and once outside, I dust myself down and cough and cough. I find my bag and take a hankie and blow my nose and cough some more.

'Sit down and keep quiet kid,' Carl says. 'He told me it was safe in a loft. Double-crossing sod. Now we need to use the metal detector in the garden. I want your word that you won't run off and in return as soon as we find the stash, we are off and you are free, though we may have to leave you tied up.'

'You promise?'

'Yeah Summer, we don't mean you no harm, after all, you are my brother's only kid.'

'OK. I promise.'

So I sit and low and behold, the clouds break and a sunbeam hits us and warms me. I undo the top of the overall and let it hang. I watch as they wander up and down with the detector. They cover the whole garden and find a rusty knife blade, a half crown that was worth an eighth of a pound sterling, an old iron pot and a sickle. That's it. They widen the search to the wild cliff top. I go to the old loo at the bottom of the garden and open the door carefully. It's not as bad inside as I thought it might be. I use the facility. I seem to be going to the loo a lot, but then I have been raiding the twelve pack of bottled water. There's paper on the roll, so someone must use this place, maybe people who could appear at any minute. I exit and look back then something strikes me. The ceiling is much lower than the slate outside and I can't think it has an insulated roof.

'Uncle Carl, can I get out of these coveralls and put my skirt on?'

'Yeah OK.' He is preoccupied, waving the detector about.

I go to the van and retrieve my skirt. I give it a good shake and then pick off some straw and chaff. I get out of the disgusting coverall and into my skirt. That makes me feel a bit more like Summer.

I go back inside the loo. I'm right. The ceiling inside must be about eighteen inches below the slates. I lower the loo seat and stand upon it, hoping I'll not descend into the cavern beneath because although this has a cistern, it's just a seat over a deep hole full of shit.

I push at the roof boards and one moves. Dust falls and I lean back against the rear wall. I look up again and there is definitely something there besides what looks like sand and bird muck. As my eyes become accustomed to the gloom I can make out details. It's a metal box with a padlock.

I jump down. I know why dad sometimes didn't want to do the beach and left mum and I to our own devices, to explore the delights of the tourist shops of St Davids and the shops of Fishguard. We delved into bric-a-brac, ate ice creams and looked at the art galleries. I remember that metal box he kept in the car, his tools he said and he kept it locked. At the time I didn't question that because when he was not robbing or on a bender, he was a labourer on building sites. I pull the boards back into position.

I walk to uncle Carl. I'm really tearful. 'Uncle please let me go. I brought you here and I can't help you any more. I've told you all I know.'

'Then you would run off to the police and we would be arrested for kidnap.'

'Not if I said I came willingly.'

'They wouldn't believe you!'

'Fucking creepy kid,' says the Gorilla. 'Don't trust him.'

'Her,' I say. 'The name is Summer. You're just a beast, Mr Gorilla.'

'Watch your tongue.' Carl says.

The Gorilla has seized me and lifted me aloft and I'm beating at him with my hands. 'I'll throw you over the fucking cliff, bloody brat.'

'Put her down.'

'Bloody kid needs teaching a lesson.'

He drops me heavily. He has really hurt me this time, twisted my arm and my ankle has gone when he dropped me.

I debate whether to tell them where the box is but I decide they don't deserve it. Their treatment of me has been rough, especially the Gorilla and I would hate to think of him enjoying eating paella in a flash Spanish restaurant on the proceeds of a robbery in which a guard was badly hurt. I picture him in pokey, enjoying porridge.

I sit myself in the sun and soak up the heat while the two idiots spread the search into the adjacent field. I rub my ankle. I think it's OK.

I've had enough of their nonsense and I don't trust them to let me go while they make an escape because I have too much knowledge.

I look over the mound that marks the border with the field. They are busy walking up and down and probing with a rod and digging with a spade. It all looks like a lot of hard work even the Gorilla wielding the spade is red in the face. Carl looks up and sees me.

'Found it?' I ask stupidly, deliberately and I expect annoying them even more.

'Fucking kid!' The Gorilla says.

'Stay where I can see you,' Uncle Carl says.

'OK. I'm going to sunbathe on this bank. It's nice and warm out of the wind Uncle.'

So I take off my jacket and lay that on the bank and try to make it look like I'm still wearing it. I think if they can see the jacket they'll assume I'm there. I walk doubled to the lane and then remove my shoes and walk briskly in my bare feet down the lane. When I have covered two hundred metres I put on my shoes and run. I cover the next three hundred metres in double quick time and I enter the little shop breathless.

'Please phone the police. I've just escaped my kidnappers.' I shout at the girl and hide behind the counter.

Chapter 14.

It is half an hour before we hear a siren and a police car arrives. In that time I've had a cup of tea, two sultana scones, a bar of chocolate and an ice cream. I sit in the small stock room out of sight with a bottle of water.

Two male police come in followed by a woman officer who has a Sergeant's stripes on her arm. She asks where my kidnappers are and I tell her at the cottage and give directions which is not hard, the first dwelling on the left up the lane. They can't possibly miss it but the siren has probably frightened Carl and Mr Gorilla by now. They will be on their way up the lane that eventually hits the main road.

Meanwhile the Sergeant checks me over. I assure her that I have no permanent damage, a few bruises is all. She takes notes of what I've experienced.

Two more police cars arrive but apparently uncle Carl has gone. There's no trace of the van and in spite of road blocks, Carl has disappeared in the maze of narrow country lanes.

'I know where the money is,' I say.

'Then you better show us.'

'OK but first I need to speak to my family. My phone is dead.'

So the Sergeant dials the number and Kayleigh answers.

'It's me,' I say, 'Summer.'

'Where are you? We've been beside ourselves with worry.'

'It's a long story, I was kidnapped by Uncle Carl looking for the money Dad stashed down here in Pembrokeshire.'

'Pembrokeshire? Where's that, in Scotland?'

'Wales, bottom left hand corner.'

'Are you OK? They haven't hurt you?'

'I'm a bit beaten up and dirty and I've been so frightened.' Then I burst into tears. God Uncle is right, I am such a girl. I sob and the shopkeeper produces a box of man size tissues.

I blow my nose and wipe my face. 'Anyway, I'm OK, just tired and filthy and I need a good long shower and a hair wash and a sleep.'

'When will they send you home?'

'I have to help the police locate the money, then I don't know. I'm OK, just filthy, tired and a bit beaten up. I think I've got to go. I'll speak later.'

'Can we speak to the police please Summer.' Ros has taken the phone.

'Yes mum.' I hand the phone back to the Sergeant. 'Mum wants to speak to you.'

There's a short one sided conversation. The Sergeant says, 'Yes,' and 'we will,' and 'don't worry Madam.' Then puts the phone away.

'Come on, You can speak later but we need to find the missing money, then we will get you to a doctor for a check up.'

So I go in the police car with the Sergeant who says her name is Jean. I show them the door the idiots kicked in and then the loo and a tall policeman easily thrusts the boards aside and brings the box out.

'Well it's heavy enough to contain something.' He gives it a shake and something moves inside.

'We'll take it back to the station and get an expert to open it. Now then young lady, we better get you to a doctor.'

'I'm OK.'

'We need to make sure, after all this is a kidnap case and if you are harmed, then they would be charged with that as well.'

'Can I phone my family again?'

She hands her phone over and from the back of the police car as we head to Haverfordwest Hospital, I talk first to Mum.

'Are you safe now darling,' she asks.

'Yes mum. In the police car on the way to somewhere called Haverfordwest for a medical, although I'm OK.'

'Really?'

'Yes mum, it's just a precaution, like they have to make sure they haven't harmed me.'

'Well I, we're driving down to fetch you back. Where are you going to be?'

'Where am I going to be?' I ask.

'You'll be with me. Let me speak,' and she takes her phone and gives an address. She passes the phone back to me and I speak to mum and give her the gist and then speak to my darling Kayleigh. By that time we are pulling into the hospital and Sergeant Jean Evans escorts me inside to reception.

We are led to an examination room and asked to wait.

We seem to wait a long time and then this young lady doctor comes in and I'm requested to change into a hospital robe. I ask them both to leave while I do that.

The doctor reappears alone and examines my top half and I'm covered in bruises, large ones from the Gorilla's punches and where he gripped so hard and a number of small ones from rolling about in the van. Then she examines my bottom half and I just want to curl up and die. So I have to tell her I'm trans and on spironolactone and give the name of my new GP. She asks if any sex has taken place and I must go absolutely puce, because she says it's OK and I'm safe. I tell her no I haven't been molested at all. I'm allowed to dress. I sigh and by the time I come from behind the curtain, I've got myself together.

Then we are off in the police car again and go to the station. They open the box and after ringing the Metropolitan Police, it's discovered that the money is intact.

I go with Sergeant Jean and she takes me to a Chinese restaurant and we have a slap up meal, no expense spared and she is really nice, especially now she is in civvies, though she was really impressive in her uniform. I love the hat and when we arrive at her home, she lets me wear her jacket and hat. I look so smart. Perhaps that's what I'll be when I leave school or college or Uni if I ever get that far. So then as I'm near collapse she shows me her shower and toiletries and I have a shower and get

175

into her spare bed. I'm asleep immediately and I'm dream free.

I wake and it's daylight and by my watch I see it's nine. I've only had two hours sleep, yet I feel really rested. I go to the loo and hear footsteps. When I emerge I find Jean there on the landing.

'Well Summer, you best get dressed, your mum is downstairs waiting to take you home.'

'She got here quickly.' I say.

'What time do you think it is?'

I look at my watch and find it has stopped. 'What time is it Jean?'

'Eleven thirty.'

'But it's still light!'

'Summer you have slept for sixteen hours.'

'Oh crikey. I must have been tired.'

'No surprising. Here, your mum has brought clean clothes for you. So have a nice shower, do your face and come down when ready. Your sister wants to come up, is that OK?'

'Of course.' I go in the shower and come out wrapped in a towel. Kayleigh is sitting on my bed.

'Oh my darling,' she says.

'Hi.'

'Are you OK?'

'Mm, still tired, I think from the strain and the threat but I'm all in one piece.'

"Here are your clothes. Do you want me to leave?'

'No, of course not. We are a couple aren't we?'

'Of course but in the past you have been really shy about letting me see, you know, your bits as you call it.'

'Oh it just feels different now, now It's real and I'm transitioning. What's here doesn't matter anymore, I mean I hate it and wish it gone, but you know what my body is like and I have to be a realist. I don't want any secrets from each other. I want to know all about you and periods and whatever else girls have going on and I'll be honest with you. I'm going to bank my, you know, oh God, sperm.' I draw breath and I hate myself for even mentioning the word. 'They are talking about womb transplants for transwomen. If that is possible, I'll go for it. Perhaps you could donate an egg in return for my sperm. Think how wonderful that would be if we both had a baby.'

'My God Summer, what's happened to you over the last two days?'

'I don't know. Somehow those two idiots made me grow up, I mean I behaved dreadfully and used terrible language and moaned and I was as much of a nuisance as I could be with two thugs. I behaved a bit like a spoiled brat, with some reason and somehow, I feel more mature after it.'

I stopped and completed my face. 'Do I look OK?'

'You look super, a bit tired, but even so lovely. Shall we go down? Mum has been so worried, well and dad too.'

'And you?'

'Of course me. I love you Summer.'

'Then everything in my World is perfect.'

We go down and I embrace mum. 'You look tired dear,' she says.

'Perhaps I slept too long.'

'No you needed sleep after an experience like that. At least they haven't caused any permanent damage.'

'And thanks to Summer, we've recovered the money. She'll get a reward.'

'I was thinking, I think the reward should go to the injured guard, after all it was my father that nearly killed him, so it wouldn't be right for me to profit would it?'

Sergeant Jean looked at me a slow smile spreading across her usually stern police face.

'No Summer, you led us to the money. Tell me, how did you know it was there?'

'Well I never knew dad was stashing when we were on holiday. I hardly knew what he did, certainly didn't know he was a bank robber. He said the box was his tools for working on the building sites. Anyway, mum and I went to the beach or into the little towns while dad did whatever. So when those two idiots took me down there, they pushed me up into the cottage loft because they thought the money would be there. Well it wasn't. Then they used a metal detector and I went to the loo. I noticed how low the ceiling was and couldn't work it out, so I stood on the loo seat and pulled a board and there it was. No I don't deserve the reward. It was my dad hit that poor man and it wouldn't be right for me to profit.'

'Quite right Summer,' Mum says. 'I'm proud of you. In any case, we don't need the money. We will look after you, that's what we are paid to do and like to do.'

Eventually we say goodbye to Jean and get on the M4 motorway for the long trek home. We stop at services for a meal. When we are all sat Mum says, 'Summer, when you were in the home, no one assaulted you sexually did they?'

'What do you mean? The staff? No I didn't see any of that, not with me anyway, but then I had a reputation. There were things going on between the kids. That just seemed normal, what happened in homes. Some of the girls were on the game, sort of amateur, part time. Sometimes they went missing and would turn up a few days later after staying with some bloke, you know, travelling salesmen staying in down market hotels.'

'Oh Summer. I'm so glad we decided to foster you. I hate to think what would have happened had you stayed there. You may have acted tough, but you were so vulnerable. If you had been discovered as trans while there, I hate to think.'

'Well mum, you're right. I don't know what would have happened. I guess I would have drifted to the bottom, like I was. Now I have my big Sis to help me and I'm on the up again. I'm so lucky to have her, so lucky that she saw something in me that made me worth befriending.'

'I was always attracted to the clean, silent, shy boy. You acted tough and most were afraid of you. I saw something else and I was intrigued. I wish I had plucked up courage to take you home sooner. I should have done.'

'Hey you are both getting really weird today. What's brought all this on.' I say because I'm embarrassed by so much open affection. That hasn't exactly been my life up to now.

'We were so worried, we thought we had lost you. Kayleigh cried most of the time.' Mum said.

'Oh darling,' I say, 'I'm so sorry, but thank you for caring for me.'

"Of course I care for you, silly girl. I couldn't work out what had happened. I stood at New Look and then sat in the shoe department for ages. Then I phoned mum and told her I'd lost you. The police didn't want to know at first and then I said your dad was in prison and they became interested. Then next day they started to trace your phone and then that went dead. I kept texting.'

'I know, I had about fifty texts but never had the opportunity to reply until I was in the loo, then the battery was flat.' I tell them of writing the message in the loo and the Gorilla standing guard outside. Then as the car drones along towards London, I flop down in the back seat and fall asleep. I'm still completely bushed. I just want to get into bed in a nice clean nightie, cuddle down with Kayleigh and have a lovely safe sleep.

Chapter 15.

They picked up Uncle Carl coming off the Brittany Ferry in St Malo France two days after I had returned to the bosom of my foster family.

I take two days off with a sick note from mum to return to school with. Over those days she makes me study three hours in the morning and then we go swimming the first day. She has bought me this bikini that has a little skirt for the bottom half, just for safety's sake and I love it. Of course I haven't much to fill the bra but I feel such a girl. Luckily for me, I am slim in the waist and actually have some hips and a bum when I poke it out. I examine myself carefully before leaving the changing cubicle.

I'm amazed that after swimming Mum looks pretty well as smart as before. Other normal people come out of the changing room looking terrible, but not Mum. True she wears a swimming hat but even so.

I settled in to the last two weeks of school and tried to work. Somehow the story went round the school that I had been kidnapped although there was no mention that I had been Summer. I don't know how the story got out but there is always a copper[6] ready to sell a story even when a minor is involved but as an under eighteen years old, I should have been protected.

---

[6] Copper, Rozzer, Pig, Bobby, Boy-in-blue, Peeler all slang for police in UK.

The second day we go to the Mall for more clothes. 'More?' I say and mum replies, 'You came to us with just a few boy clothes so you need to catch up with Kayleigh and you are not having her hand me downs like a little orphan Annie.'

So she buys me more undies as well as some beach/holiday wear, and bits, a nice necklace and some bangles and nail polish. I had no idea girls needed so much stuff. No wonder one whole floor of the biggest Department store in the Mall is devoted to makeup and hair accessories. The Gorilla is still at large and I fear that he might even yet come after me for revenge. We hadn't exactly been the best of mates and the news media had reported the recovery of the stolen money. He would surely bear a grudge.

Last week of term and I come home with my school report. Mum receives Kayleigh's and of course hers is all super, top in nearly everything except strangely, history where horror of horrors, she is only fifth. She can't make it out and nor can I because I would think she has a dead hand from sticking it up to answer teachers' questions.

I slink out of the kitchen while Kayleigh's examination by mum is going on and I think I will escape my own interrogation. I am changing into girl mode when Mum shouts up the stairs, 'Summer, your school report please.'

No one has ever demanded my school report before. I used to bin them on the way home from school. I just wonder what sort of treatment I'm going to receive when she sees it. I haven't even opened mine, afraid lest it is worse than last time. I have been getting better marks but then I don't know what other kids are getting do I? It is of course all relative. If the rest of those around me have also improved I could still be twenty-four out of thirty one in the class or maybe thirtieth. I don't believe I can be thirty-first because that place is the preserve of Robert Simpson, known as Simple of course.

I finish dressing and do my lashes and eyeliner, even though I'm going nowhere. I grab the envelope and go down to find my fate.

'Mum, here it is.'

I wait for her to be angry or something and Kayleigh watches from the doorway, ready to jump in to my defence I think, I hope anyway.

'Eighteenth out of thirty one. Where were you last time?'

'Twenty-fourth mum. It's much better isn't it?'

'Yes Summer, but not good enough is it?'

'But in the last half of the term Mum, since Kayleigh coached me, I've improved so much.'

'She has mum, she has really worked hard and life hasn't been easy for her has it? I think she's done really well.'

'Yes I can see that. I do think you've done well Summer but I want to see you do even better next term which is GCSE year.'

'Yes mum, I really hope to.'

'You are not a dunce Summer and I expect you to go to Uni so just buckle down. Is there any coaching you need because if need be, I'll find a tutor.'

'I think I have the help I need in Kayleigh. She's the best teacher ever and I do her orders in payment mum. That's right isn't Kayleigh.'

'You don't have to do anything in payment, we are just sisters helping each other. It works OK mum. She's really trying and now she's happy, she's doing better.'

'Very well. We'll see what happens in the autumn term. Now we need to think Summer and think carefully. Are you going back as Summer or Peter? Don't answer yet. Think it through, talk it over with me and with Kayleigh. If you think you can go on leading a double life and you want to, I say if you want to, then that will be OK. If you want to transition full time, then that is what you must do. From the point of view of the psychologist or psychiatrist, they would be more convinced if you transition full time. But if you do, there may be difficulties, bullying, snide comments, well you know better than I the bullying that takes place. Are you strong enough to transition? You will need to be strong. Of course whatever you decide we will back you.'

'Mum. I think I want to transition. I'll think about it over the next week.'

'A decision preferably before term end would help, then I can speak to your headmistress if necessary.'

'OK mum. What you said about being my half sister or cousin? Really I thought about that and I don't think it would work.'

'Good girl, I thought about that too, and it was my idea but I don't think it would work either. Just think about it and talk when you want to.'

'Yes mum.'

'Come here.'

I obey and think what now, have I a dirty nose or have I suddenly developed facial hair or what. I stand dutifully before her and she takes my face in her hands and kisses my forehead. Instant tears, not blubbing, but tears of joy that I am at last treasured and loved and someone actually cares whether I pass or fail. I put my arms around her and kiss her cheek in return.

'Right off you go and do your homework. Dinner in an hour.'

That's how it is, Mum really cares, I mean not just that I am dressed and clean but the state of my mind and my future, like I'm her real child.

We sit either side of Kayleigh's table and work away and I have tears in my eyes and Kayleigh, my minder sees and says, 'Whatever's the matter?'

'I'm so happy,' I say. 'For the first time I have a family that really cares whether I do homework and how well I do in school. I just love being here and I love you Kayleigh for seeing something in me and asking me to be your companion.'

'You are becoming a very sloppy girl, but I love you for that too.'

I finish my homework and she tests me on the fifty chemical symbols we've been instructed to learn. I do well. She then reminds me that I have a history chapter to mug up. Well that should be easy because I like history, it's just like a story. We go down to dinner as soon as we're called and it's a favourite of mine, something that I would not have eaten three months ago, liver and bacon and Mum has this way of making everything so tasty. We have proper baked potatoes with it, baked in the oven so the skins are crispy, even slightly burned. I always take out the inside and leave the skin for last. Then I put butter salt and pepper and it is delicious.

We finish with fruit, fresh, peaches and cherries with ice cream. Mmm. I'm living like a Princess when three months ago I was just a homeless waif. It's a fairy story come true.

So I clear the dishes and switch the dishwasher on and clear up as it's my turn and then I take my history book in the lounge and read that chapter for the test tomorrow, Henry the eighth and the dissolution of the monasteries. Craft old sod, it was about robbing the church of it's Wealth and of course, there was nothing wrong with that really because just like the nobility, the Roman Church oppressed the people and took a tenth of any crops they produced as well as being land owners. The book tells me that the Church deliberately kept the people God fearing and ignorant because that way, their way of life continued. Fat priests and starving poor, just like in Robin Hood except of course that Robin was a composite of a few outlaws of his time.

We watch a love story with mum and then it's bed and every night we, Kaleigh and me, sleep together. It's a given and we chat about school and people and the holidays.

We are booked to go to Brittany and Mum got me a passport and she has used a perfectly frightful photo of me, yes as a girl with makeup, but I look so grim. Still it does say female, because mum figured that I would be all girl in the holidays. She had to get doc to sign the thing and photo.

Anyway now it doesn't look like Harry will be coming, because of the emergency and him being counter terrorism. I have mixed feelings about that. I mean he has been OK and sort of relaxed about the trans thing but I still feel it is different with men, like they think I've joined the enemy. See men, boys can't even think about wearing pretty. Mum says it was only in the eighties that men started wearing pink, first a shirt that might have a thin pink stripe, then pink shirts but in a manly fabric and now they even wear pink trousers. Daring. I guess someone like my dad would call anyone wearing a shirt and tie a poufta or the other name is twink in UK, meaning a small framed girly man. Anyway I look a lot up on the laptop now, in fact when I want to know anything. And what I read is that a lot of men thing MtF transwomen and girls are just gay, homosexuals, bum bandits. I despair of men. So I got off the point there didn't I? I'm a bit glad as well as sorry that Harry won't be with us, because I don't think he will understand.

With a lot of women, they understand, because in their minds, wouldn't anyone want to be like them? Except and ain't there, isn't there always an except in life, except that ultra feminists are against us, as though we are going to take over the house of femme. I don't get people. They are so effing strange. See I'm even swearing like a lady.

That's another thing. After being a boy for fourteen years, it's real hard to throw off all that conditioning, all the hard leather exterior I had used to disguise the real me inside. That's another think Kayleigh does for me, she pulls me up. I don't mean that I'm mannish but sometimes a bit high spirited and then I can use words that a nice girl wouldn't. I want to be a lady, like Mum Ros is.

Chapter 16.

'What do you think I should do?' I ask Kayleigh.

'Well if you transition and go back as a girl in September, it will be tough but I'll be there for you and Sally and Jeanie, we can depend on them and there's also Liz, Em and Rosie. We can count on them too I hope. I can't tell you what to do, this has to be your decision. Just remember what mum said, about the doctors being more impressed that you're determined, if you are halfway there, living full time as a girl.'

'Oh gosh, it's crunch time. I think I know what I'm going to do but I have three days to make up my mind.'

'Do you know Summer, you sound more posh everyday. You used to be a bit Estuary[7] now you are sounding more like me.'

'I'm trying to, pronouncing my aitches and my gees and tees. I want to be an upmarket girl.'

'Bless Summer. Just proves something to me, you never really know someone just by casual acquaintance. Like when you were just a boy in class, three months ago and now, well look at you and listen to you. By the way, did anyone say anything about your ear studs?'

---

[7] Estuary is a name given to a particular down Market southern English accent prominent in the Thames estuary area.

'Yes Keith said it was poofy and when I said about Lewis Hamilton, he said he was a poof as well. Martin tried it on and I reminded him that last time he took a rise, I kicked his manhood.'

'Oh Summer, I hate that you have to behave like a boy. They are so rough with each other. No wonder you want to be a girl.'

'That's not the reason is it. It's everything, like I don't want to be rough, I want to look pretty, I want pretty clothes and I want to relate to the rest of the World as a woman. It's quite different in so many ways. You need to be in my shoes to understand how great the difference is.'

'I think I'm beginning to understand but this is not a conscious decision, I mean not a decision at all really is it? There is something inside you that is female and driving you to shake off the boy, compulsion not choice, compelled by what makes me like being a girl and dada like being a man.'

'You got it.'

End of term came at last and now I could be a girl full time. The first weekend and as usual Ros was off to Davina on the Friday as soon as we had been picked up from school. Ros says in the car, 'By Sunday you need to know whether you will go back as a boy or a girl Summer, So think, chat and discuss. I know it's a hard choice but you have to bite the bullet if I am to speak to the

Head and she will have to speak to the Governors and the other teachers and maybe, the PTA.

'Yes mum. I think I have already decided. I have thought about it a lot and discussed with Kayleigh and she hasn't persuaded but this is my decision. I'm transitioning, I'll go back as a girl.'

'Well now. Then next week I will put the ball in motion and we will have to get uniform for you unless you wear Kayleigh's as she seems to have three of everything. You still have thirty-six hours before I will demand an answer.'

We kiss mum farewell and off she goes to her exciting life in London with her Davina. We are free with no homework, school over until September and seven weeks of freedom between now and the start of the Michaelmas term.

We cook our supper. Mum has left us steak and we make chips too and I demand frozen peas and Kayleigh chooses runner beans that are fresh and from our own garden, the only veg that they grow. We prepare everything between us and we even make a sweet, taking two pears from the fruit bowl and poach them in red wine and Demerara sugar.

Kayleigh to my surprise, lays the table in the dining room and when I look the silver candelabra is on the table and the candles lit although of course, being high summer, it is full daylight. There are glasses by our place settings and the ice bucket on the table and resting in it a bottle that looks like champagne.

'What are you doing?' I say, shocked because we never drink.

'This is a celebration of making the decision and I thought too, a celebration of us, Summer and Kayleigh. Our engagement party and then I am going to take you up to bed and we will have the best time.'

We finish cooking, and it is a lovely meal though the chips are a bit soggy, not crisp on the outside like I wanted them. The pears for afters are great and Kayleigh holds my hand as we sit and sip our bubbly. I am quite tiddly after one glass but she pours another and I'm having trouble focusing.

Somehow we manage to clear the table and we feed the dishwasher and she makes sure all the doors are locked and windows closed. She leads me up stairs and I feel as apprehensive as a bride. I don't know what has brought this on nor where it's going. In the bathroom she strips me and I feel terribly exposed and vulnerable. I wonder how she knows all this stuff, the seduction and the treatment of me as it is so different to what we usually do, falling into bed when we are tired and messing with each other. This is more deliberate, more planned.

It is silly but I feel afraid as well as excited. I want her to do whatever she wants with me. I am completely in her power and I'm pleased to be so and yet, apprehensive.

For the first time she touches my down below as we stand in the stream of water. Somehow, whether it is the effect of the alcohol we have consumed or just that my mental state is such, nothing happens. My penis stays limp and I'm at least grateful for that. That thing that until now has had a brain completely it's own fails to stand up for itself.

She dresses me in a nightie that is diaphanous and white and brushes my hair and I don't want her to stop. She leads me to bed and has undressed herself in a couple of minutes and is beside me.

'Your bridal night,' she says and laughs and I hope this is not making fun of me.

She is not. She bites into my neck just as an appetiser and moves her lips to mine and then to my neck and down my body. One hand fondles my left breast, her lips play with my right and my body goes taught as a spring. My down below is straining for release from the confines of the panties and I use a hand to trap it between my thighs. I don't want a third party getting in on the act. I try to relax and I do to an extent, but her lips and hands are travelling all over my body and I want her to stop and yet I want her to continue. I am in ecstasy except that damn thing keeps trying to get in on the act.

She takes my hand and teaches me what to do for her, leading me from lips to breasts and her rib cage and it is her turn to taughten and arch her back. I'm urged to go ever lower, move my lips ever lower on her body until I reach her special place and the juices that I find. I don't know how long we spend in making love but at the end I am exhausted and I think, she is fulfilled for she pulls me to her, turns me and cuddles into my back her left arm lying across my back and her hand upon my pathetic tiny burgeoning breast.

'Thank you,' she says. 'I have truly welcomed you to the sisterhood. I hope you will never want a man.

'Oh God no,' I say.

I fall into sleep having truly joined the sisterhood. In the morning we cuddle and she teaches me more, moving my hand taking my finger to circle her nipple guiding my mouth to suck. I am her slave and she reciprocates, trying to find my sweet spots and I find my nipples are erect and sensitive and most sensitive of all my lips that almost send me crazy when she caresses with soft fleeting kisses. I cling to her like a koala to a eucalyptus, so hard that often she has to stop and then I beg her to start again.

Eventually hunger drives us to get up and we shower together. I love it but try to hide my man bits, pushing my gonads into their little pockets and stuffing Willy Dangler between my thighs and holding it there by the sheer muscle power of my thighs. It's horrible, this deformation that I have to live with. I feel I could deal better with having part of a limb missing than this hated male organ between my legs.

We dress and decide to go to the Mall, not really to shop but to browse. We both have more than enough stuff, and to keep buying more of the same but different seems pointless. We have enough so that we can ring the changes and swap clothes between us, so that a top will go with a skirt, the combination new though neither garment is.

We turn a corner and there before us are Sally and Janie, the inseparables, the girls who enjoyed the joke of leaving me holding hangers of girlie undies.

'Hi,' they say in unison, and I manage to stay mute, answering with just a smile.

'Hi you two,' Kayleigh says, 'what are you up to.'

'Just browsing. You?' They appear not to recognise me and I see sly shy glances as they wait to be introduced.

'Do we know you?' Sally asks looking at me with a slight frown. 'We've seen you around haven't.....? Oh my God, Petie?'

'Summer. My name's now Summer. We best go for a coffee and I'll try to explain what's going on.' I say, for once feeling confident. We walk to Fresh Ground, the new coffee bar that offers larger coffees for less money.

We order and sit in a little booth by the window that three boys have just vacated. An assistant clears the table and wipes down.

'So Petie, Summer what's going on?' Their faces are alight with interest. Funny isn't that anything to do with sex is so attention grabbing, not to just these two girls but to all in the so called civilised World but primitive peoples seem to take so much, including deviations from the norm as normal.

'I'm transitioning, coming back to school as a girl,' I say, 'so that time when you left me holding the underwear wasn't so funny after all.'

'Oh Christ, we are so sorry. If we had known, we would never have played such a silly joke. Petie, Summer I mean, honest we would never have.' Janie says.

'Hey it's OK, I guess when we get back to school it will be a lot worse. I look forward to a lot of bullying, a lot of whispering. My reputation as a small thug will be ruined forever.'

'So what brought this on? Was it living with a girl, you felt jealous of what she had? Is that sort of how it works? I don't know anything about sex change. Is that what it is?'

'Yes that's what it isn't. No it was nothing to do with living with a girl although I do sort of idolise my dear sister Kayleigh who is such a brill friend. And it was her that recognised in me the girl that lurked inside my boy body. I have felt I should have been a girl from when I was tiny, five or six but for various reasons, my dysfunctional family being the main one and then being in a home, it was never the right time. Now I'm in a stable and loving family, I was able to admit to Kayleigh and then her mum how I feel, and I have seen a doctor and I've started treatment that will eventually result in me becoming a woman.'

'So what are you doing about school?'

'Returning as a girl in September.'

'Oh my God Summer. That will be brave. Aren't you terrified.'

'Well my street cred as a pocket sized thug will be long gone. I know the idiots will have a go and they will try to make my life a misery but I'm depending on the more intelligent to try to understand and to help me.'

'It's a brave choice,' Janie says.

'Not a choice,' say I. 'It's a compulsion. I just can't face spending the rest of my life as a boy and of course I feel natural and happy, much happier as a girl. There is a force within me that I cannot resist. It has been there from my earliest memories and cannot be denied. I have to do this or spend the rest of my life unhappily. I can't change how my brain thinks and therefore I have to change my body.'

'I still think it's brave, whether you are compelled or not.' Sally says.

'It is really brave. She is really brave,' Kayleigh says. 'It's good we ran into you two because we need your help to you know, protect her at school. You know what the idiots are like, Martin and his sort already have it in for her when she was Pete. Now they will have a field day. We can't let them win can we?'

'Rather not. You so look the part Summer, I mean when we first spotted Kayleigh, I didn't think, there's Petie in drag, I just saw a rather attractive girl with her and thought, who's she?'

'Thanks girls.'

'So what happens now Summer. Are you having drugs or something?'

So I fill them in on what I have to do but of course I leave out the gory bits like operations and I don't tell them about using part of the colon for a vagina, I keep it simple. I feel for me it is no big deal, I mean becoming the person I feel I should be is the big deal, getting there may be hard, may be horrid, but that is something that just has to be borne, a method to achieve the end, something that will be endured to become a whole person.

I have read a lot recently and the new methods have so improved results, they at last give trans women more sexual satisfaction than they ever experienced in the past.

We finish coffee and decide to see what films are on. We walk the length of the Mall and take the escalators up to floor five and the entrance to the cinema. There is so much rubbish on. In the end we select the best of a rather poor lot, a film without monsters that is also not too childish. There are so many good stories, so many great books but of course, making them into films might involve some great direction and acting ability, so why not make a cartoon, CGI is so easy, no stroppy actors to pay a lot to, no royalties or minimal amounts for a voice overs and out comes what is really a pulp film, great for kids but bad for everyone else. I have only just come to that conclusion.

Anyway we see this film that is rated fifteen and it is not too bad. We come out and go for pasta, the four of us. Then it's home time. We haven't bought anything, not even makeup and I feel very self-righteous for being so good and restraining my desires for ever more girlie acquisitions.

Chapter 17.

The next week I dress in jeans and a T shirt and looked as androgynous as possible and Ros takes me to see my mum. It's something I dread and I had been told that for months she hasn't wished to see anyone even when I'd phoned which was pretty seldom.

She's now feeling stronger and has asked to see me. I wondered why, after so long, she has asked, has remembered that she has a child. Poor mum, but also poor me. I'm not being self-pitying but although I have great sympathy for mum and the way dad mistreated her and was the cause of her breakdown, I lost both my parents, my dad who I now cared not a jot for and mum, making me a penniless orphan and consigned to the child dump, the local children's home, the place that breeds no hopers.

It is by a stroke of luck that I have found a new home after two false starts with foster parents, at a time when I was so disturbed. I didn't appreciate what they were doing for me and I had to learn and abide by their rules. That had been a hard lesson to learn but I know it now and think myself lucky that first Kayleigh saw something in me that attracted her sexually at least and that her mum saw a boy who was worth saving.

So we drive to what is laughingly called the psychiatric hospital, underfunded, staffed by no hope doctors and a few dedicated nurses and some who are there simply because they forgot where they had laid their ambitions.

Mum Ros says she will wait in the car and to ring her if I want her to come in and meet my poor mum.

I go in and I'm immediately struck by the smell a mixture of disinfectant and other indefinable smells, none of which combine to make a nice odour. Odour, that is an ugly name for the ugly smell that is enough to raise goose bumps. I feel intensely sad. My poor mum. I love her so, still and if I could I would hug her well and we would walk out of there together ready to face the World. Unfortunately, I cannot work miracles and few happen in this sad World.

I find mum in one of the day rooms watching a repeat of a soap, one that I would never watch because every character in it has cheated or lied or worse. It's enough to drive anyone into a fit of depression.

Anyway mum sits there and I have to kneel before her before she registers that it's me.

'You need a haircut.' She says and I don't know what to do. If I tell her what's going on with me, she will maybe go into a spin and I don't want that. My poor mum, once so pretty and vivacious, beaten down by my no hoper dad and the shame he brought on our small family and the pain he inflicted on her by his rough and violent ways as

203

well as his unfaithfulness. She must think that God has deserted her.

'Mum, I wish you could get better mum.'

'How's your dad?' She asks as though I care or would know.

'I don't know mum, he's away isn't he, you know that, locked up in jail for hitting that guard.'

'How are you looking after yourself then?'

'I'm living with a friend from school mum. I'm doing OK, getting better marks and I'm happy mum.'

'You look different Peter, you look like a girl, you really do.'

'Do I mum? Is that a bad thing?'

'It is for a boy. It's dangerous. Get a haircut won't you. I wonder your dad hasn't made you.'

'He's in prison Mum. You remember don't you?'

'He's not all bad, your dad. We had some good times. He was a lad, your dad, before you were born. The tricks he got up to, the presents he brought me. I never knew what next. How long's he in this time?'

'He got life mum, killed that guard.'

'Oh yes. Serve him right. He had a terrible temper your dad. Promise me Peter, you won't be like that.'

'No mum. I promise I won't be anything like him.'

'What are you doing now?'

'Still at school mum. I'm living with this lovely family who really look after me and I have a sister, not a real sister mum but I'm loved and looked after.'

'You talk like a girl.'

'That's because I am one mum. I'm going to be a girl mum.'

'That's good dear. Just stay out of trouble, don't be like your dad.'

'I won't be. Mum I wish you would get better, for me mum, I want you back.'

'One day dear, just now I don't have the energy to look after you. You so look like my sister. You should be careful looking like that in our rough area. Now I think you should go, I'm rather tired Peter. Come again won't you?'

'Yes mum. One day and mum, promise me you will try to get better.' I realise she has switched off. I don't know whether it's her brain or the dope they pump into her that has made her a zombie. Perhaps she really can't face the real world and lives a twilight existence, her brain flitting from one elusive memory to another, rambling from fact to imagination.

I exit the place and walk to the car where Ros and Kayleigh wait patiently. I open the door and sit in the back. 'Let's get out of here,' I say.

'How was she?'

'Rambling, in a dream World divorced from reality. She said I look like her sister. She died in a road accident when she was nineteen.'

'Oh dear. I'm sorry I wish you hadn't that problem.'

'Perhaps one day I will have enough money to look after her properly.'

'You really need to concentrate then on doing the best for yourself, don't you.'

'Yes mum and I am, now I have a new family and I have a brainiac to help me. I feel so lucky that you've taken me in.'

'We are lucky too. You are the sibling Kayleigh always hankered for and you love each other. That is really more than we could have wished for.'

'You are both more than I could have wished for, so we are all blessed.' I say.

We arrive home to find Harry there. He looks dead beat, asleep on the settee two empty beer bottles of his favourite designer brewery on the floor beside his sleeping form. We reverse out and let him lie. Mum closes the door quietly and we go into the kitchen.

'We were having a family holiday in the West Country, in Devon at Saunton Sands but I don't think Dad will still come. Do you want the three of us to go? If so, I may if you approve, ask Davina down.'

'Of course mum,' Kayleigh says.

'What about you Summer?'

'Me? Of course it's fine with me. How could it not be as long as she respects what I am.'

'Oh she does, she thinks you very brave.'

'I don't know about brave, it's just something I'm compelled to do or go under. I wish people would stop saying brave. It's just what I have to do. I'm lucky that Kayleigh happened along that day to rescue me. I know that may sound over dramatic but it isn't. I might not be here, I mean in the World, had she not come then. I was feeling pretty desperate.'

'Dear Summer, thank you for saying that. I have felt a bit guilty, because sometimes it feels as though I have pushed you in a certain direction.'

'Oh yes you bossy pants, you didn't push, you shoved, but it was a shove in the direction I wanted to go and I will always thank you for that and for getting me out of that stinking children's home.'

'I can't imagine the pain you have endured Summer, with your dad and your mum, the home and your state of mind, your dysphoria. I don't know how you endured all you have and still remained a really nice person. That's what I call resilience. You have real inner strength.' Mum says.

I burst into tears, their praise bringing emotions to the surface that I normally manage to keep submerged. They both hug me and I recover and I begin to cry giggle, my sadness and past experience all mixed up with my present joy at being a girl, in a loving home with at least two people that really value and care for me.

'Well I will wait until Harry wakes and then we will know whether he has time off or whether we go without him. It will be a shame if he can't come because he values the family holiday, the only time he has with his daughter and he does love Kayleigh deeply. He also has admiration for you Summer. In spite of all the disadvantages in your life he admires the fact that you have risen above them.'

'Oh Gollywogs. Oh I mustn't say that must I. My Gran used to say that. Oh crikey, I've never received such praise, but it's just something inside of me that gives me that strength. It's not that I have made a conscious decision, it's a basic human trait, a basic animal sense of self-preservation. Even insects have that instinct, like a fly tries to escape the swat.'

'Yes but as far as we know, animals and insects don't have the choice, don't have the sense of hopelessness that drives us humans to commit suicide, so your analogy is way off Summer.' Kayleigh says.

Later in bed, we just cuddle and discuss. 'You do really love your dad?' I ask her.

'Oh yes I do. Even though sometimes he is here so little. He wasn't always like he is now. When I was little, he was such a doting Dad and he is generous in spirit as well as with money. He only wants the best for me and is delighted that you are here to keep me company.'

We go to sleep cuddled up, me into her back like we are a couple of spoons. Her hair smells wonderful, fresh scented from her shower before bed when she washed it.

Chapter 18.

In the morning when we awake, I hear the murmur of voices from bellow and know that Ros and Harry are discussing matters and the family being as it is I have no wish to interrupt. At least their voices are not raised so whatever they are saying is not spiteful and destructive.

I turn and find Kayleigh watching me and I'm going to speak and she puts a finger to my lips and says shush. 'I'm trying to listen to them,' she breathes.

So I lie and listen too and watch her face. I can hear conversation but no real words, Harry's lower tone and mum's higher. I feel guilty listening in but I say nothing. In the end I think we are none the wiser but not Kayleigh.

She gets up and therefore so do I. As she passes on the way to her bathroom to relieve herself, she whispers, 'They were talking about you, nothing bad that you have done but something's bugging them. We best get ourselves down and see what's going on.'

So we do what we have to, the loo and a quick wash and a brush through our long hair and we go down in our nighties and slippers. We enter the kitchen and find mum laying the table for breakfast and by the look of things the 'full English' is on offer, which in this house is eggs and bacon, maybe a banger,[8]fried bread and fried tomatoes.

---

[8] Banger, slang for sausage in UK, from when in wartime, they contained so much bread they burst their skins.

'Mm yummy,' Kayleigh says. She kisses her dad and sits herself on the big man's knee, an arm around his neck. 'Long time no see dad. Has it been awful.'

'Pretty grim,' he says. 'These mindless and repugnant madmen. As fast as we arrest them more appear. It's a battle we keep pace with but can't ever win. It's frustrating. It means I will only have four days with you at Saunton Sands but let's make it the best we can. We can teach Summer to body board and land yacht. Then I will have to get back to London.'

'There's something else too Summer. Your dad is out, escaped when he was on the move to another prison because they thought he was planning an escape in the Scrubs. They were moving him to the Isle of Wight and the van was rammed. On the way to hospital he escaped the ambulance.'

'Oh golly. I didn't have anything to do with it.' I say defensively, feeling guilty and ashamed.

'Of course you didn't but it means that he is on the loose and he might turn up here or track us down. Would you want to help him?'

'No fear I hate him for what he did to mum and then his two henchman kidnapping me. Never fear I would turn him in if he ever came near. He ruined mum's life and he could have ruined mine had I not had a bigger problem to solve.'

'Sorry Summer. This is not what you wanted to hear at all is it. Mum and I were wondering what to tell you, if anything. In the end we thought better to have no secrets and we don't keep secrets in this house. I know you are aware of our marital differences and all that, but somehow it all works and we are happy and the home is stable for you two to grow up in. I'm glad you and Kayleigh are so happy together, so don't be bashful about that. If you two want to hold hands or whatever, it's fine by me. So we will have four nice days at Saunton and then I have to get back to searching for and arresting toe-rag terrorists.'

'Sorry dad,' I say, 'it would have been nice if you could be with us longer. I hardly know you, you have been so busy. Is it awful in London?'

'It's pretty grim. The state of the victims, breaks your heart and the worst thing is, they are perfectly innocent people just out leading their lives, some of whom are actually Muslim. This hateful ideology of militant Islam has no logic, no religion, just pure hate and the people that indulge in it are all in need of psychiatric help.'

'Daddy, come on. That is all banned for the next few days. We'll have a happy time at Saunton at least. Can't you possibly stay longer?' Kayleigh asks her father.

'No darling. We are spread too thinly as it is. We have raids on suspects everyday and one raid leads to another, wider and wider as we connect up all these people.'

'Breakfast is ready everyone,' Mum says and thrusts plates on to the table. 'After breakfast, pack your things and we are going today rather than tomorrow while daddy is off. It means we may have to change hotel rooms but that can't be helped. So two cars and you two think who you are travelling with.'

'I'll go with dad mum as I see him so little.'

'I'll keep you company mum,' I say.

'Thank you dear,' she says.

So we pack and Kayleigh, bless her, helps me pack and thinks of things that I wouldn't, like accessories and all my toiletries and even tights in case we want to look smart. I just thought beach stuff, jeans, shorts, minis and tops, flip flops and sandals, but there is far more that we need because the hotel is smart and we also go to upmarket restaurants. There are people who go there at the same time every year, so there is a bit of competition between different groups, a bit of one up-man-ship, out-doing the other. So the few bits of designer wear all go in our cases. We take tennis rackets, bats and balls, beach balls a kite and even dad puts in some quite manly looking beach spades because he likes to build a huge sandcastle. That is another area of competition. I don't know Harry very well but I've just found out, he is very competitive in just everything from his golf to sandcastle building.

The journey is long and Mum talks and teaches me about behaviour as a young lady and I realise it is more for my benefit than not letting them down. I just want to pass, to be a girl and respected as a girl rather than a fascinating oddity. I'm a willing pupil and ask for more and more information and Mum Ros doesn't mind talking about personal things like periods and menopause and using pads versus tampon, not that any of that is going to be in my agenda after I have had surgery, more's the pity, unless of course womb transplant becomes possible, but the accompanying female anatomy as far as I know it, and five months ago I knew nothing, would all seem so complicated that a surgeon would have to be a wizard to make it all work. After all, many natural born women have all sorts of reproductive problems that can't be solved by the surgeons scalpel.

I read once an Italian doctor was planning a head transplant, from one body to another. I don't think that ever happened, but he had thought it possible. If so it would be the answer, because it is this boy body that I hate.

We stop before the turn off from the M5 motorway, for a snack Mum says but dad seems to have a very large snack. I suppose a big man needs to have a huge intake of food to keep that huge frame energised.

After what seems a very long trek, we arrive at three in the afternoon in gorgeous sunshine. We are taken up to our rooms and find that we are in lovely adjoining rooms overlooking the beach and about a hundred feet above. The golden sands seem to reach in a straight line for miles with sand dunes on the landward side and the great Atlantic Ocean beating upon it. The beach is three miles long and ends in the River Taw estuary with the town of Westward Ho beyond. Appledore is just up river, a place where they build small ships. We face west, so we should have the benefit of the setting sun if we are lucky enough to have good weather.

We two half unpack and Kayleigh is in a hurry. She tells her mum and dad that we are going down for a swim. They promise to follow and they will find us. We change into our bikinis, mine with the little skirt that I hope hides you know what and the top that badly needs filling.

In flip flops and carrying towels and two body boards, we run down the hundreds of steps, more like two ten year olds than two girls soon to take their GCSE exams.

I lose a flip flop and it sails over Kayleigh's head as she is first and lands in some sort of bush but we manage to retrieve it and we make haste more slowly afterwards.

We cross a small and suspect stream that flows from the cliff and take off across the sands until we find a patch of firm and dried out sand that is free from other holiday makers. We dump towels and after creaming our bodies with protective, we head for the waves with the boards. I expected the ocean for some reason to be warm, but it isn't very. We head in, Kayleigh leading and she sort of teaches me the theory of body boarding.

At the first attempt, I swallow a mouthful and spit it out in disgust. I hadn't realised the ocean tastes so disgusting, so salty, I say and she is so surprised that I didn't know.

'Well I've never been to the sea before.'

'What never Summer?'

'No, well we went to Southend and went on the pier and on the little train, but we didn't ever go in the water.'

'Oh crikey girl. I hadn't realised this was all so new. You can swim?'

'A bit, because in juniors we did have trips to the swimming pool.'

'Well don't go out of your depth, ever. Look the board has a lifeline, that should go around your wrist and tighten like so. The board will keep you afloat so you never leave it, it is your safety belt. You are more deprived than I ever thought. All the things I take for granted, you have never had. I have been so casual about things and I didn't realise how hard your life has been. I have been so wrapped in enjoying your conversion into a girl and loving how you have liked it, I have been selfish in my enjoyment, hardly thinking of how difficult everything was, not just the mum and dad thing and the home but everything. I'm sorry.'

'Don't be. I don't want that. I'm happy now and that's down to you too and that is what counts, the friendship and love and sharing you have given me. I will be eternally grateful. So let's not think about the awful past but concentrate on the now. So we wait for a good wave and do we set off before the break or after or just try to time it on the break?'

'We try to catch it at the peak as it breaks so we are sloping down slightly. Not this wave look there's a bigger one coming. Beside me and launch, now.'

She is gone riding down the wave on her tummy. I'm left, hardly moved. I try the next and the next and then finally I catch one that moves me twenty or so feet. By that time, she has waded back to me and we try together again. I sort of get it and over the next hour I improve but I find it frustrating, waiting for the perfect wave and I can see one coming and then to suddenly it becomes quite tame and the one that you ignored turns out to be the biggie.

When we've had enough, we float ashore and make for our towels. Ros and Harry have arrived. Even undressed he is an impressive man I mean big and muscular, a real man who has really worked out it seems. I would not like to be the criminal or terrorist that he feels the collar of. I bet he could be rough.

I was quite frightened of Harry, after his threats about having sex with Kayleigh but now he is as gentle as a lamb with us two, especially Kayleigh who he seems to worship and his love for her splashes over me too as her chosen friend. What's more he gets my name and pronouns right and I'm just his prospective adopted daughter and his daughter's beloved friend. He puts an arm around us both as we walk the beach towards Westward Ho which of course we can't reach for the river. On the way back we find an abandoned beach ball and we run and kick at that and laugh and giggle all the way up the beach until we reach mum who lies soaking up the last of the afternoon sun's rays. For an older woman, over forty, she has a lovely body. I wonder Dad can even look at her without choking, wishing she was still his instead of being the sweetheart of Davina. Still he has his own love in his London flat so I guess they have worked out a relationship that suits them.

We all lie in a row, Mum, Kayleigh Dad then me.

'Dad,' I say, 'we were sort of thinking about when I have my operation and where and I was thinking like Thailand, because it's cheaper and they have done a lot of quite famous people and developed new methods that I don't suppose you even want to think about. Anyway, I suggested we all go the four of us and the girl friends, Mum's and yours, I'm afraid I don't know her name, oh yes Samantha. It would be two weeks of lovely holiday, the whole family. I would be in hospital for about five days as I've read and you could all just take turns to come and spend time and then we would have time to see the sights before I'm finally discharged and we all return to England.'

I have gabbled all this in an endless stream and no one has interrupted. Everyone is sitting up by now and I think I have caused an upset but then Dad chuckles and pulls me to him and gives me a kiss on the cheek and ruffles my damp salty hair.

'You really are a girl aren't you? What a nice plan. Are we even sure yet it will be Thailand? Wouldn't it be safer on the NHS here in England?'

'There are one or two surgeons there who have a really good reputation, Kayleigh and I researched it, and I just thought, you know, you and mum have your own romantic attachments, there are no secrets as far as I know and we know that you both have found happiness that suits you. It would be so lovely to be altogether a sort of extended family, everything in the open including me.'

'You are a sweet girl Summer,' Mum says resting on one elbow and facing me, her dark spectacles perched on the end of her nose so she can look clearly at me. 'We will have to talk about it and see but it is a nice idea and we thank you for making the suggestion. Maybe though we can find something in this country and it's looking into the future a little isn't it, after all, you are not yet on oestrogen. You can't hurry this process although I know you would want to. It's a long journey and it can't be rushed but I promise you this, I will do my best to get you along the road in as quick a time as is reasonable. You have to be assessed and medicated and they will not give oestrogen until you are sixteen, so that is months away.'

'I don't even like thinking about it,' Harry says, 'even hearing about it. You have to be awfully desperate to do this.'

'Yes of course Daddy,' Kayleigh says. 'If you were a girl but thought like a boy as you do now and liked boy things and felt natural as a boy, you would want to get on with things wouldn't you?'

'I expect I would. I can't imagine someone my size wanting to be a girl though.'

'They do dad. It's nothing to do with how you look, size or anything, nor wanting, it's just making the body fit the mind isn't it Summer?' Kayleigh says.

'Yes oh wise one.' I say. 'My brainiac sister.'

Chapter 19.

Over the next days I get closer to Harry and find he's not such a forbidding character after all. He is concerned for me, worried that *his* daughter has had undue influence and he asks whether that is so, quietly while the two of us are standing alone on the harbour side in Westward Ho.

'No, I have always had these thoughts and this sadness within me, that I was not happy being a boy and thinking that I should have been a girl. I'm jealous of girls, not just Kayleigh. It's not even jealousy, more envy, that girls have the things I want, starting with dress but appearance and attractiveness and body shape and how other people see me and mannerisms and vulnerability as well as emotionally. I look at a girl and I look from top to toe and I think, well, if they are lovely like Kayleigh, I wish I was them, like having a romance with a boy and children, babies, just everything. Whereas a boy looks at a girl and just wants to, well give her one, you know, possess her for a while or for life. I want to be like that girl. You see the difference.'

I see Kayleigh and her mum leave the toilet and instead of walking towards us, they walk to a few shops selling souvenirs and art works, using art in it's broadest sense.

'Oh yes Summer, I see. You really are a girl aren't you. So my darling daughter has done you a favour by bringing you out?'

'Yes Harry, the biggest favour you could think of, like if she had jumped in the river to save me from drowning, it would not have been a greater service to me.'

'I'm relieved we've had this chat and I understand a bit more, much more, where you are coming from and what you need. I'm pleased that you've found in my lovely daughter a true friend and a lover?'

I blush. 'We do kiss and cuddle, but that's where it stops. My downstairs is definitely off the map, not to be seen and not to be touched. But yes, I really love her Dad. Who knows what will happen in the future. She may find a boy that she loves. In a way I hope she does, for if she finds a way to be straight rather than a lessie, life I think will be so much easier for her and so probably more rewarding. I'm going to bank my sperm, just in case I find a woman who wants to have my children. That was doctor's advice and also mum's. I hate discussing that though because it's so boy.'

'Poor girl, so many hang-ups, so many yet to be solved problems. Life isn't easy is it?'

'No and with my Mum in the psychiatric and Dad on the run. I hope he doesn't turn up at ours.'

'I looked at his record Summer. Not nice reading. Let's find those girls.'

We walk and meet them coming towards us. So we make our way back to the hotel and this is dad's last night.

We have a lovely dinner and a bottle of champagne, the first I have ever tasted and it's OK, I think a bit like bitter lemonade, so what's all the fuss about. What a disappointment, but what a lovely happy foursome at the table. I find it hard to believe that the parents really lead separate lives because they appear to get on so well and are outwardly loving without a cross word.

In the morning we are just the three of us. I ask whether Davina is coming and I'm told that it is rather a long way to come just for a day as she is still in the play and that is doing good box office. I think that's the phrase mum used.

Anyway we amuse ourselves on the beach and try to get a glamorous tan that I fail to do with my fair skin and mum lathering me with sunscreen. The result is that by the end of the holiday, I have just the faintest glimmer of tan, so if I lower the straps on my bikini you can see where they were but you would need a magnifying glass and a UV lamp. However, I do have a healthy glow mum says and I should be satisfied. My eyebrows on the other hand have turned white and I buy some dye to give my face some definition. My hair too has lightened and I wonder whether to colour it. Mum says no but I say yes and Kayleigh agrees. We buy this one that says dark blond and actually it does make my hair darker without looking dreadful. Mum passes no comment.

After the two weeks we are in the car and home and I am gloriously happy but dreading my monthly visit to hospital to see mum, when that is allowed. These visits make me really tearful, distraught thinking how horrible her life is.

She isn't fit enough this time I'm told. 'Come if you feel you have to but we would not advise it at this time.' That's what they say. There is the dichotomy, a word that I think I have used correctly, taught me by Mum Ros, meaning two ways. The dichotomy is that I hate seeing mum in her state and feel guilty for not seeing her. Ros says that it is probably worse for me than mum, because she is away in her dream world and numb, while I am in the real world and hurting. She gives me a big hug and oh God that is so comforting, to feel her warmth, her arms wrapped around me, possessed and cared for and protected. My eyes are moist.YY

I get my second dose of T blocker. It hardly hurts, just I sit a bit carefully for a couple of days but I am free of the fear of turning into a hard muscled and hairy teenager. That is such a relief after all these years of fearing male puberty that sometimes kept me awake at night a snivelling wreck in my bed, the covers pulled up around my head to contain the sobbing.

We go to Brittany, driving all the way to Plymouth for the ferry to Roscoff. This is a really big adventure, like we are in this big ship that has shops and two restaurants and big lorries and cars, and it takes hours to cross, I mean no land in sight.

We reach France and it's sort of like England but the houses are different, lots that are sort of like dormer bungalows with windows that come out of the roof. They have lovely gardens with lots of flowers and window boxes even in the towns and on bridges and roundabouts. I thought England was the country of gardeners but France was lovely. And the beaches, just hundreds of them with free parking and clean sand and plenty of room, not like Southend or even Saunton, just so much space and we could have a beach all to ourselves. We stay in this cottage that also has a pool and we swim a lot and I feel more confident swimming, I even do a length under water, just holding my breath.

We eat lot's of ice cream and fruit. I also eat lots of seafood, creepy creatures that I never guessed could taste so good. Mum makes me try everything and I learn not to turn up my nose because these creatures have shells or whiskers or pincers or for any reason unless it is the taste. So I eat and enjoy mussels and chips, fiddly but nice, and langoustines and lobster and crabs. I try snails but that really is not my dish and also an oyster. No not for me.

We return to UK. Dad has still not been caught Harry tells us. That is a cloud that hangs in the middle of my otherwise clear blue sky. The Gorilla has not been found either. I wonder whether they have teamed up and Dad has found out that I showed the police where to find his loot and that he now knows I'm a girl. Well I don't owe dad any loyalty after what he's done to my mum and he hasn't been much of a dad either. I guess he will not understand who I am now. I don't care whether he does or not, just as long as he leaves me alone and keeps his distance.

Mum tells me she has received a letter from school and they will welcome me back as a girl in September. That is so exciting and yet so terrifying, see another dichotomy although of course the die is now cast. With that knowledge we shop to buy me school wear, all new for mum says, she wants me to be one of the best-dressed, neatest girls in school.

We take a morning and go into town to the two approved shops. There are two standards of uniform, natural fibres expensive and synthetics cheap. So I have little cotton blouses and wool mixture pleated skirts. Kayleigh advises on everything, especially shoes. All undies under our white shirts have to be white so that means new bras and chemises but pants apart from games ones can be any colour. I decide on black and the pants are as plain as we can really find for school wear. I have real pretty ones for out of school. I am soon kitted out. I will make do with her second best hockey stick and she says, she has enough tights to last till we get to sixth form when we can wear our own dress.

We go to a couple of parties, a twenty-first, the daughter of Ros's best friend Carina. It's a big affair, a band and disco and we are asked to dress pretty so we both wear mini dresses. Kayleigh has this great red lace dress and shows eight inches of brown tanned thigh. I have a blue dress, sky blue in a silk and polyester mix that also shows a fair amount of thigh.

Leanne from school is there and I try to avoid her but Kayleigh says, 'I won't have you hiding in a corner. You have to face the World and face it with pride. Many with your problems have gone under, you haven't. Be proud. You can't help being the person you are.'

Anyway, I know she is right but that knowledge doesn't make it easy. My sister adds, 'Look if people don't understand and accept then there is something wrong with them, not you.'

So I'm getting another drink when Leanne arrives beside me. She looks pretty, long blonde hair and in a real pretty dress that hugs a perfect figure. She looks really sweet and she says with a smile that shows perfect teeth, 'Do I know you, sure I've seen you somewhere.'

Here goes then I think. 'Wallace, I used to be Pete at school, now I'm Summer. Going back as a girl in September.' I say with what I hope is my most bewitching smile.

'Oh crikey, so you are! Oh my God!' She is open mouthed in astonishment and I can see her eyes roving over me. 'That's a brave choice.'

'No it's who I am. There's no choice. I always have been a girl, just with the wrong body. It's been horrible, pretending all these years, trying to be who people expected me to be. I'm exactly the same person but now I'm dressing to suit my being, my brain, my self.'

'But you always had such a rep. You floored Gangle Martin and Mike Lee.'

'Stuff my dad taught me, teaching me how to be a boy like him.'

'What do your parents say?'

'Mum doesn't know what day it is and doesn't care. Dad was in prison for robbery. That's how it is.'

'She lives with me now.' Kayleigh has appeared beside me after watching from the other side of the patio where she was talking to a boy. I had felt jealous that a boy was chatting her up.

'What like sisters?' Leanne asks.

'Definitely sisters. Yes I love her. I think I always have and I think I always knew the real person behind the disguise.' Kayleigh reaches out and takes my hand. 'She's really beautiful and such a girl now the disguise is off. So Leanne you can spread the news, it will save us explaining.'

'I don't tittle-tattle. I won't tell if it's a secret.'

'No we want you to tell. Everyone will know when I go back to school in a skirt anyway. I'd like it to be old news by then Leanne. That's a lovely dress. Where did you find that?'

'Miss Selfridge. Do you really like it Summer?'

'I do and you look like you've had a good holiday. Where did you go?'

'Our family and the Gramps go to a small place in Cornwall. We love it there. I think Paige Austin from our class is coming to the party and Justine Clarke. Shall I tell them?'

'Tell who you like. I'm not hiding.'

'In fact we are having a party for her, sort of coming out, so you're invited Leanne and if Paige and Justine come and say hello, they're invited too. In fact text me your email and we'll send email invites, by invitation only, not open house.'

'Boyfriends allowed?'

'The invite will be for two, so bring a friend, boy or girl.' Kayleigh says.

So it's all arranged then. I'm having a 'coming out' party. I'm furious that she hasn't spoken to me first.

I pull her away into the garden. 'Kayleigh, what are you doing to me? A party?'

'Hush darling. Come.'

She takes my hand and we walk away behind a hedge that hides the vegetable garden. She swings to face me, still holding my hand.

'You need to be pragmatic, logical. Everyone is going to find out so better we give them the right message, the story we want them to have rather than the one put out by the gossip mongers and, this way we get a load of people on side, so when you return to school, you will have more friends than just me. You can't hide now, it's too late and you are not going to revert to being that miserable Peter are you?'

'No, just it's so daunting. What about mum and dad? Will they allow a party?'

'I will manage them and yes, they will. We'll have it on a Sunday say starting at four, a barbeque and drinks and you will say a few words and that will be it.'

'Easy for you, this is really hard for me, coming out in front of all these people and school and kids that don't want to understand and who hate anyone who is the least different. Look at Jamie Thomas, who just has a bit of a squint and how they bully him.'

'Yes but doing it this way, having a coming out party, you will get people on side, because they will know and not imagine things and they should be your friends because they have eaten and drunk at your party. It's got to be a better way than pretending hasn't it?' Kayleigh is so persuasive.

'Kayleigh I know you're right, just that on the day, I'll be absolutely terrified.'

She put her arms around me and kissed me. 'Poor frightened little tough guy. Have you always been frightened of people and the tough guy was just a protective image?'

'Yeah. I was always terrified that I would be seen as a sissy, queer, I dunno, anything other than straight and normal. That's why I occasionally dropped someone like

Martin and Mike Lee. Those occasions sort of put a fence around me and put people off the scent as well as keeping them at a distance. I knew if anyone got too close, they would discover how wimpish and girlie I am.'

'Except I saw the good in you.'

'Are you sure? When we met that day in the Mall, you said, 'what are you up to, no good I'll be bound'.'

'Oh did that hurt? I never realised you were so sensitive, but then I wouldn't would I, because you had cultivated this aura of the tough guy who didn't care about anything much, like having mates or being liked or having pride in your schoolwork. The only thing was, that although your uniform was sort of like second-hand it was always clean and you were always clean and I stood behind you on the stairs and I could smell your hair that always looked nice, and I knew you had used a good shampoo and conditioner. Your finger nails too, were always a fraction long for a boy and shaped a bit, not like the ragamuffin kids with nails chewed to the quick, and another thing, you had no cuticles growing down your nails like lots of the boys, the half moons showed. There were just so many signs that contradicted the image you cultivated.'

'Are you going to be a detective like your dad? You must have put me under a microscope or something. What made you so interested?'

'I don't know. What does attract you to someone? There is just that magic, that sort of lightening strike. It may not be love at first sight, just that a face, a movement, a word or tone of voice, attracts. You were my mystery to be solved, my attraction to be unravelled. I'm pleased I bothered.'

'I'm pleased you bothered too. Just one thing that worries me. Instant attraction sometimes fades when the person behind the façade is known, properly known. I'm terrified that I won't come up to scratch in some way, that you will discover you really are attracted to boys, or want a real woman.'

'Oh honey chile,' she said, lapsing into her Mammy speak from 'Gone with the Wind,' one of our fave films, 'I love you and the more I know about my little frightened brave rabbit, the more I want to caress and cherish. I fear that when you are fully a girl, some boy will sweep you off your feet and carry you off on his white charger.'

'What's a charger?'

'A war horse, like knights of old, King Arthur and Sir Galahad and all that.'

I laugh as I picture myself in a long flowing blue dress, hair to my waist flowing in the wind, a gold coronet balanced on my hair and a gold belt circling my impossibly small waist.

'You are already my Sir Galahad, or Lady Galahad.' I say.

'You do really like me then Summer? It's not just what I have done for you that has made me sexually attractive, you like me as a person too?'

'I wouldn't say that, I mean what you have done, turned me inside out, how could I like you? I don't like you, I love you Kayleigh. I'm a better person and happier because of you darling Kayleigh. I do really matter don't I? I'm not just a project, like your business.'

'My business? You don't compare to that. That buys me and you nice things and I want to make a success of that just as much as I want you to be a success, but I can't see that happening without you by my side and we must get down to work tomorrow. We better get back to the party and I bet the news will have gone around by then.'

We walk back into the garden and I see Paige and Leanne and Justine in a huddle with some other girls and a couple of boys, one of whom I recognise as being in the form above.

'So here you are, you two. What have you been up to in the rhubarb patch? I was just telling the guys about Pete being Summer.'

'Oh that's good,' I say, full of bravado, 'as long as they are getting the right story and not some garbled account.'

Paige comes forward and kisses me once, on the cheek. 'Wow, you really look the part Summer. So you give us the true version.'

So I tell the group about trans as I know it from the web, about things happening in the womb, about genitals and the brain not developing at the same time so if mum has an excessive flow of testosterone or oestrogen at the wrong moment, or antigens stop flowing, variations happen that make brain and genitals out of sync in the foetus. So it's the same as a child being born with any deformity, like hair lip or as they call it, cleft palette, or legs that are bent or any multitude of other birth defects. It is just that sex as defined by gender seems so much more important to people than any physical deformity. I tell about this tribe in Central America, where girls are born who turn into boys at puberty, caused by some local lack of mineral in their food that I can't remember and then I tell about those lions in Africa, where the females look like males with a mane and they take on the male role in the pride.

'So I'm pretty normal, just that humans in our society have this thing about putting everyone in a box with a little label that says, straight, gay, lesbian, trans, or a mixture of any of them and about seventy other classifications. I bet you are all bored by now and so am I. I just want to get on with being the person I am inside.'

'I get it,' Paige says. 'You're all right Summer. I know someone else that's trans, going the other way. It's a pity you just can't swap bodies.'

'As long as she has a nice body,' I say, 'curvy with long legs.'

That does get a laugh after what has been a serious moment. Leanne kisses me and Justine looks shyly and says, 'You are brave though. The little tough guy image was actually more genuine than we even thought.' She kisses me on both cheeks.

'Thanks. Anyway, I'm hungry after all that. Is the food ready?' I see it is and we form a queue to get a bread roll that feels like an eiderdown and with as little taste, some half burnt cheapo burgers that probably contain thirty per cent meat and some of that will be horse's ears, and some sausages that look like burnt slugs. Luckily it tastes OK, except for the bread roll, but the fried onions help that down. One helping of that is enough, after all I have to look after my figure. I move onto the gateau and then an ice cream, a Cornetto choc nut.

Mum comes over from where she has been with the grown ups. 'Are you OK Summer?'

'Yes mum thanks.'

'I saw you holding forth. So you are well and truly out?'

'Yes mum. Your darling daughter made me see the light. She is truly a remarkable young woman, old beyond her years.'

'You really love her don't you?'

'Oh yes mum. Worship as well. I would die for her.'

'Let's hope it doesn't come to that. Did you know that Mr Grainger the school head is here? Come with me and say hello.'

Well she has my hand and I can't resist. So off we trudge, me in my little sparkly platform sandals and the mini dress showing six inches of thigh to meet the head. I mean the head is a daunting figure at any time. I put on a brave smile.

'Here she is, our Summer who you knew as Peter Wallace.'

'Hello Sir,' I say.

'Hello Summer. Well I would not have known. I saw the pretty vivacious girl who had the rapt attention of the group and I wondered who she was. Well done Summer, we shall see you again in September. If you have any worries, don't forget to see the school counsellor or come and see me or the deputy headmistress. We are all rooting for you, so work hard. I won't have any bullying or nastiness in my school.'

I thought, well it is already there, rampant but everyone turns a blind eye. Suspend any bully immediately and perhaps it would end.

'Yes sir, thank you sir.' I say.

Kayleigh has come up by my side. 'Paige has invited us to her party next week,' she says. 'I said we would be there. Mum I want a coming out party for her before we go back to school. Sunday week would be good.'

'I'm in London with Davina, all Friday and Saturday.'

'Yes mum. I'll arrange everything. You will just be there on the Sunday to make sure order is maintained and perhaps you should invite one or two parents, grownups? Even Mr Grainger?'

'Yes dear, if that is what you both want?' She looks at me for confirmation.

'Yes mum. I think Kayleigh is right. I shouldn't hide. It's like having any other birth defect. Best I be out and proud.'

'There is no shame Summer in being who you are. That is something you cannot help just as you cannot help being white or coloured or black. It's something you are born with. So let's get things in the open and when everyone has the facts, perhaps there will be no bullying.'

Chapter 20.

So she, who must be obeyed, my companion, lover, counsellor and teacher goes about organising my party which will be as chance has it, both birthday and coming out. I shall be fifteen years old, the week before I go back to school as Summer Wallace. We have also been wracking our brains over a second name and she has come up with Sky. I think it's kinda silly and reject the idea. Then I think and say it to myself enough times and actually I quite like it. Summer Sky Wallace and then I think Wallace, that's dad's name when I hate my dad for all the best reasons so my mum's maiden name was Somerville. Summer Sky Somerville. Eureka. Oh yes it is a bit fanciful but there are the children of pop stars who have much more ridiculous names.

I tell Kayleigh and then I tell Mum Ros and she questions me about it and my reasons and why I have rejected completely my birth name and we decide to do the thing properly and change by deed pole that costs a little fee, but is I think, worthwhile although you can in UK, call yourself by any name and just tell the authorities. Mum and Kayleigh and I do it all on line and it's dead simple. I will have a new medical card in that name and also a passport and everything else in due course, like a driving licence if I ever get one.

Meanwhile the party invitations have gone out and Kayleigh has asked for any presents to be shopping cards at three stores selling girl stuff at reasonable prices and has put a ten pound maximum, which I think is sensible and fair.

Ros asks whether she should put anything at all, but as usual, Kayleigh has so much logic on hand and argues her case so well that that's the way the invitation is sent. That way I will not get anything I don't want and yet people do not have to spend a fortune. At the end I may have a hundred to spend on clothes.

I decide that I'll wear my sky blue silk and polyester shirtwaister for the party. The colour suits my eyes and it's quite understated, not overly feminine, but defo girl, and I will wear sandals with three inch heels and the pearls and crystals on the strapping. Harry says he will be there if he possibly can be. I hope he comes because I have begun to warm to him. I know we don't see much of him but he is a proper dad and he treats me as a girl, teasing and cuddling and sometimes advising when we see him.

He is still busy. He says that chasing terrorists is never ending and every raid leads to other terrorists and he is afraid, knocking in someone's front door may make other terrorists, the final bit of white British oppression as they see it that turns some Muslims to be violent in return. I hope he's wrong. I wish people could all just live in harmony but the human animal is not like that. Whether it is Muslims hating white people and their personal freedoms, particularly things like female liberties, or those that hate for other religious beliefs or gay-bashing, or those who ignorantly poor scorn and hate on trans, there is really no good reason for disliking anyone because they are different. Muslims hate the kaffir as they call us. In my mind, religion encourages hatred when it should, if one boils it down to the essence of a faith, encourage love of others of whatever shade, creed, or sexual persuasion. Would a real God if there were one, ever want a person or persons to be crucified for their difference as long as that difference does not harm others? Why do Jews and Muslims hate each other so, when they share the same genes, same God and the only real difference is the Prophet Mohammed. Mankind has a long way to go before becoming truly civilised and bombing and killing proves that.

Three months, no nearly four months ago, before I sort of emerged from my male chrysalis I would never have thought that deeply, because then I was so wrapped in my fears of discovery and being trapped in my male skin from which there seemed no escape. I owe Kayleigh my life. I don't think she will ever understand that, nor even though she loves me, can she fully understand the pain I suffered.

Anyway, the weekend of the party arrives and of course we two are on our own Friday and Saturday. So me and Kayleigh string the party lights on the patio and we have borrowed garden furniture from all over. We checked the gas for the barbeque and during the week mum bought the sausages, chicken bits, prawns and some upmarket burgers and we are instructed to buy baguette loaves not those thin and weedy batons, that every one thinks is a baguette. We will make a salad and we have five pounds of strawberries to prepare plus we have plenty of cream and ice cream. There is beer, red and white wine and elderflower cordial and juices.

So mum doesn't get home until eleven on Sunday morning and we are starting to panic that she won't be here to welcome her friends. When we hear her tyres scrunching on the gravel we are so relieved. Harry has phoned to say he should be with us by three, four at the latest and he will put his chefs hat on for the barbeque. Why men always do the Barbie, I don't know, but that seems written into the culture of western folklore. That of course includes the English speaking people of the Antipodes another word I have learned from brain box. I don't mind who does it and mum is really good at talking to people just like Kayleigh, and dad can do man talk with any that turn up. There are fifteen kids from school and some boyfriends and the rest are neighbours and friends of the Dawson's, well principally Ros's friends because Harry doesn't seem to have any close buddies, not even at the golf course where he has given up the captaincy because he has no spare time in the emergency generated by the latest idiotic, pointless, hateful barbaric acts in London.

What is heartening is Harry tells us, that London is normal, not under siege as President Trump tweets. A man in his position should not tweet because once something is out there it's out there. He should consider before he utters these remarks. Trump shoots from the lip before his brain's in loaded. Actually they should take away his phone because he just likes acting as a naughty boy and a bully.

It's the kids who arrive first, the girls are all sweet and kiss me and the boys just try a smile and a sort of hand shake followed by a grunt. All the time, Kayleigh is by my side like a real partner and says things like, 'Let me introduce you to Summer Sky Somerville who used to be Peter Wallace.'

Richard Danes, a clever clogs asks whether that was Peter as in Peta or did he hear right, Petra. And I say no, Peter as in Pan and I'm a girl and not a boy and I want everyone to know how happy I am with my new persona.

'Are you being funny or just being offensive,' my guardian Kayleigh asks rather too defensively.

'No just she looks so nice, unbelievable.'

'Thank you Richard,' I say. 'Please help your self to everything.'

I whisper to her, 'It's OK. Don't defend me unless it's really necessary.'

Most people are really fine, some a bit too interested and some, even grownups, embarrassed. That's interesting.

No one says it's immoral or anything like that, so that's OK. Janey is really sweet and gives a hug and holds on and Sally too and they both claim that they discovered me and while they were all in the changing room that Saturday when we met in the Mall, they discussed me and thought me quite girl, not effeminate, camp, but sort of well naturally graceful. Kellie another girl from school suggests, 'Yeah,' she says, 'like well not really like a boy and not a bit like his reputation.' This goes on as a general discussion like I'm not there. The boys sort of don't say nothing, I mean anything, something else Brain Box has hammered into me, like I now know that's a double negative, don't and nothing together.

Harry arrives in time to do the barbeque and is soon in his nude female apron and nearly burning stuff that mum has precooked. That's the first time I see her cross with him. She just says sharply, 'If your going to do that, do it properly Harry. It is cooked it just needs flaming not making into charcoal.'

'Sorry,' he says, 'that's man trouble, can't multi task, cook and talk at the same time.'

By six there must be fifty in their garden, on the patio and the lounge and some on the lawn and luckily it is the best day of the week for weather that has been freakish even for England. It's a nice late August day about an even twenty-four degrees and staying warm into the evening.

Even so, I am cold with fear, my speech weighing heavily. Kayleigh and I worked it out between us and I hope it says everything.

'Come along Summer,' Mum says, 'Kayleigh says you have prepared a few words, so I will bring everyone together.'

So they gather and I gather my spirits and bless, Kayleigh stands one side and Harry the other, his hand upon my shoulder and mum does an intro.

'Friends and neighbours,' she says. 'We are celebrating Summer's fifteenth birthday and what she calls her coming out. I will leave her to explain.'

I realise that I have now to step up to the plate and swing.

'I never made a speech before so this will probably be a lot of nonsense, My name is Summer Sky Somerville and I'm here with the Dawson's because of a family tragedy that I needn't elaborate on. Is that the right word? I think that's what my lovely sister Kayleigh taught me to say. Anyway, until just a few weeks ago, I was a boy called Peter but I always felt I should have been a girl, like my brain said girl and my body just wasn't, so I had what I now know as gender dysphoria. That means that life felt hopeless and unfulfilled as a boy, eternally grey and unattractive. It seemed that the future would never be happy.

'Because mum was ill and dad away, I couldn't tell them how awful I felt, but dear Kayleigh saw through my disguise and brought me into the light and taught me that there was no shame in being what my brain tells me I should be. I'm harming no one by changing my gender, so no one should fear me or hate me for it. It's me that has to feel the pain, deal with the rejection of those who will not, for what ever reason, understand and it is me that suffers the medication and the surgery involved that will make me happy enough to continue living.

'I am the same person as before I gave into the compulsion of my mind. It is not my choice, who would by choice select a future that I know will include discrimination and vilification, surgery and lifelong medication? My defect is caused by something that goes amiss in mum's womb and I pop out with a brain that's girl and a boy body. It is as much a birth defect as cleft palette or club foot, but much less easy to rectify. So here I am, now starting the next period of my life with a wonderful, beautiful family as Summer Sky Somerville.

'I know that there are religious people who think what I am doing is a sin and they like to quote scripture written by some man thousands of years ago, a

247

man who thought the World was created in seven days, a man who believed in the garden of Eden and that the World by his reckoning was just six or ten thousands years old. The people that wrote those things may have been very clever in their day, but they were ignorant by today's standards. We emerged from little creepy crawlies from the ocean depths, from the cocktail of gases and enzymes that existed. We were not made of clay by God's design. We have evolved and are not perfect like coins from a mint. We are all different. Vive la difference. Thanks for coming. I, oh God, I really have done it haven't I?'

Everyone laughs and claps and Sal and Jane and Leanne and all, kiss and hug and mum kisses and dad too.

'Very well done Summer!' He booms. Then addresses the party.

'For my part as a policeman, I knew very little about this until having Summer live with us, I found out. She is a wonderful girl, and a great sibling for my wonderful and delightful and clever daughter. I love them both.'

So that's it, job done. I'm out and lots come forward to wish me well but only one boy dares embrace me, who I found out is called Georgie Motson and not at our school but away at a public school somewhere in Oxfordshire.

Come ten o'clock, everyone has disappeared and we are left with the clearing up. Harry has taken off back to

London. We decide tomorrow will do for the clean up and mum locks doors and we go to bed.

Chapter 21.

Morning dawns and we all muck in to clean up and the three of us have it done in just over an hour except for the giant barbeque that needs some special cleaning stuff from the camping shop down the road. Dad keeps it somewhere but we can't find it.

Mum gives me five pounds and tells me to skip down there and get this magic formula stuff from the camping place.

I'm walking back feeling like the cherry on the cake, the crown on the Queens head, top of the tree when I'm seized by the arm. I swing round expecting some twit from school and find myself face to face with dad. It's like for me, waking up and finding the devil beside me.

'Dad,' I say, 'what do you want?'

'Fucking look at you. What the hell Peter. Why are you doing this to me?'

'What do you mean. I'm doing nothing to you.'

'I'm so ashamed of you. That's not how I raised you. God almighty, there's enough like you in prison. It's gone round the prison already thanks to Carl. I'm a laughing stock. Some come to my cell wanting me to be their girl friend.'

In spite of the shock and maybe it's hysteria, but I laugh. I try to shake off his arm.

'Let go my arm dad, you're hurting me.'

'You're hurting me.' He mimics and if there is anything I hate it is being mimicked.

In that minute, I hate him as I have never hated anyone before. 'A son of mine, wearing effing panties. Christ.'

I shake myself free and instead of cowering, I turn towards him. I know he can slaughter me, he knows all the moves a street fighter uses, but surprise may at least be on my side, so I swing the plastic bag containing the plastic bottle of heavy duty oven cleaner and hit him across the side of the head and poke two fingers in his eyes and then I run, but not home, I don't want him invading my home and harming Ros or Kayleigh, so I run down a road that is parallel to ours and hope he doesn't know where I live. I dash in a garden through to the back and over a fence into the garden behind. Then I'm off down that road and I have my phone out and I phone the police.

'Emergency, which service do you require.'

'Police,' I say.

'What's the problem please dear?'

'My father is an escaped prisoner and he just grabbed me and I hit him and ran away. I don't want him to hurt my family.'

'Your name please.'

I hesitate, then I use my old name. 'Peter Wallace. My dad is a bank robber known as Jimmy Wallace.'

'Where are you now Peter?'

'Hiding in a garden in Park Avenue it's off the Purley High Street. It's number thirty something.'

'A car is on it's way. Stay there Peter, they will be with you shortly.'

I stay crouched down in a rhododendron bush and listen for a police siren. After about five minutes I hear the wail of the siren coming nearer and nearer and I think it has entered the road so I come out of the bush to go out into the street and flag it down.

At that very moment, A hand clasps about my face and I'm thrust down hard into the earth in the shrubbery and dad is whispering, 'Keep quiet you little faggot.'

I can hardly breath because his hand covers both mouth and nose and I try to tear at his fingers but he's mighty strong and I'm puny in comparison. Something else that worries me is that I am down in the earth and my nice skirt and little top are getting spoiled. I start to fight afresh but to do that, I need oxygen and I'm not getting much. That's the last I remember for a few minutes, for when I wake up from the faint caused by lack of air, I'm lying alone on the earth and he has gone. I emerge and look for the police. The car has stopped way down the road and I run down the hill towards them. I hammer on the window and an officer opens his door. He looks at me in astonishment..

'What's the trouble Miss?'

'I phoned you about Jimmy Wallace. I'm his son Peter but now called Summer. He had me pinned down and I fainted. I think he's run off. I'm frightened he may be with my family and hurt them.'

He comes out of the car and looks at me as policeman do, with that look of threat that says if you are messing with us, you'll be sorry. He opens the rear door and I sit in. It doesn't smell nice, I suppose from all the fellons, drunks and drug users who have been in there before me and probably puked over the seat.

'Which way to your home?'

I guide them back up the hill and then across till we come to the Dawson's house.

'Wait here Miss.'

An officer goes to the door and another stays with me in the car. Another police car arrives so there are now four policemen on the scene and I hear more sirens in the distance. Dad has been given fair warning of police presence then and If I know anything he will have made his exit from the area.

So eventually I'm escorted indoors looking dishevelled and distressed. Tears have tracked down my cheeks. Mum orders me upstairs to wash and change and Kayleigh comes with me.

I quickly shower and put on the dress that Kayleigh has put out for me. I quickly do makeup and we go down again.

The officers take notes and a woman Sergeant has appeared too. There seems plenty of tea on the go and I have a cup thrust at me for in British folklore a cup of tea cures everything including shock.

I give a statement and then mum gives a statement too saying why I live with them and what is going on with me, and why I'm dressed as a girl.

So then the police begin to depart but one car sits in the driveway with two officers sat chatting and one smoking, the smoke curling out of the car window.

We sit and watch a pop concert on TV and then a film. For tea we have yesterday's left overs but it's all good stuff and I recover except that I am quite tearful.

I'm sent to bed early with a little pink pill that mum says will help me sleep and I do. I must sleep nearly twelve hours , so when I wake it's nigh on eight in the morning. My darling Kayleigh sleeps beside me and I burrow into her. She smiles and flings an arm across me and kisses my nose.

'How are you Summer?' She asks, still heavy with sleep.

'I'm OK, I thought he was going to kill me or you.'

'I don't know, we send you to the shops for one item and then you come back with no money and no shopping. Just hopeless aren't you? So unreliable.'

I start to half cry half laugh and we cling and she wipes my tears with a paper hankie from the box that is at the side of her bed always.

'I'm sure they will soon catch him and you'll be safe again. What did he want anyway?'

'I don't know. It sounded like he was having a hard time in prison because the grapevine, thanks to uncle Carl, had said his son was a trannie. I think because of that his reputation as a hard man has collapsed. I know it wasn't out of love for me.'

'Perhaps it was a sort of love. He just can't deal with it like normal people. It's something completely foreign to his understanding and of course in prison, anyone like you would be a target.'

'I know. Unless a transgender person has been through surgery of some sort they send them to a prison according to their birth gender, so someone halfway through the process with tits and a penis would go to a male prison. Those poor devils often have such a bad time they commit suicide.'

'I never knew that.' She says.

'Oh yes, four suicides last year, and if you break the law as a transsexual, the doctors may think you unstable and discontinue treatment. It's a mess. One trans person was taken from a male prison and put in a women's and had an affair with a woman prisoner and that was supposedly wrong too, but changing sex doesn't mean automatically changing the sex one is attracted to. People just don't understand at all.'

'I had no idea. How do you know all this?' She asks surprised.

'I just read everything about being trans. It's a hard read and a hard path and a Government that hardly helps at all. All the concessions in law of our treatment have come from the EU, the European Court of Justice and the European Court of Human Rights and the Directives of the EU have forced the UK government to grudgingly give us a legal status, including things like pensions and insurance and work rights. The UK Parliament was content to pay for our transition via the NHS but refused to recognise us in our new gender. Trans people have had to fight their way through the English Courts and then take their cases to Europe. I have no respect for Parliament.'

'Summer! You never fail to amaze me. You were this dull kid in class who lingered near the bottom in everything and yet you know all this stuff that no one else does. Most people our age don't even think about Parliament or law or civil rights. They think about pop music, reality TV, sport and passing exams and clothes and fame.'

'It's my area of special interest isn't it, has to be and things are a lot better now, because some old trans people have fought for our rights. The Government gave nothing, any right trans have has had to be wrenched from the Government by laws of the EU and the European Convention, that fifty-two per cent of the nation now want to tear up. They don't know what they are doing, they really don't and the good done by the EU outweighs the bad.'

'You should become a lawyer Summer.'

'I'm not clever enough.'

'I think you are, now your brain is happier and less muddled. Think about it, think what good you could do in civil rights, feeling as you do.'

'I'll think about it. It would be a goal to aim for. At the moment I have no goal. My only wish was to be female, my basic need I should say and all my thoughts were on that, achieving that somehow. Now I'm on the road, I should set myself a new goal shouldn't I. I'd like to help people not just trans.'

'Think about it. I'm sure you could get to that dream if you wanted.'

'What are you going to do?' I ask.

'Oh commerce for me, preferably in my own company or working for one of the multi-nationals. I know I will make enough money to support my law student partner though.'

'Kayleigh, I really love you. Would you really do that, support me through University law school?'

'Of course. It would be a pleasure to see you succeed and achieve. I can think of no greater reward for me, and the money I'm going to make. For me the hard-nosed business-woman, it would be my way of giving back. So I might have a less good car, maybe instead of a Ferrari I would have a Porsche or even an Audi TT. So what. They only get you from A to B in roughly the same time and in the same comfort, but I would be supporting my lovely lawyer. I would just love to be at your degree ceremony, see you in cap and gown, kiss you in front of everyone.'

I stop her chatter with my kisses and my hand is burrowing into her panties and rests between her thighs and stays in her most intimate region and she cannot speak either and I slowly open her and caress. She is so juicy and I need to taste again and I lower beneath the sheet that covers us and look at her fantastic body and feel her smooth like silk, skin. I taste and she is sweet and she moans softly and writhes and I am her slave and she is mine, to pleasure each other in body and in spirit.

Chapter 22.

We hear next day that father was caught while trying to steal a car in Croydon Whitgift multi storey car park. I breathe a sigh of relief that he is caught and will no longer be a threat. They are sending him to a more secure prison and he will now stay in for the whole of his sentence. When he emerges, he will be over fifty.

I have my third testosterone blocker. My breasts have come to a bit of a halt but they are at least there and await oestrogen to make them bigger. Another year and I hope to be on hormones. I cannot wait. I talk about buying on line and my lover counsellor stays my hand.

'No Summer, don't even think about it. I know you want to get on with your transition but you just don't know what you are getting. The pills those people supply could be chalk or even poison.'

It's OK for her, she has breasts, she has a quim, she has in her body everything she wants. I'm dragging about this horrid male body that feels so foreign, so not me and I avoid seeing myself full frontal in the mirror. From behind, I do look quite girl and especially in this age when the hour glass figure seems a thing of the past, girls are more straight up and down than they used to be, but generally have larger hips than boys and of course most unless unlucky, have breasts. If I get a good size B I will be happy, perhaps even a C cup, no bigger, I mean what for? I saw some bras that were size H. God almighty, they would almost fit a cow. No size B would be my ideal and I hope for a bit more hip than now, and a nice bum. I was looking at photos of these West Indian girls and they had such beautiful rounded bums. That would be my ideal. I tuck my balls up and tuck Will between my thighs and look in the mirror and Imagine how I will be eventually.

Anyway, no good wishing. I come to breakfast and mum is there and she says, 'Summer, tomorrow we have an appointment with a private gender consultant in Brighton, so make sure you know what to say, get your thoughts in order and stand up for yourself.'

'Yes mum. Thank you. Do you think if I ask really nicely she will give me oestrogen or progesterone?'

'No Summer, not until a years time. When you are sixteen. It's early days, and we do this by the book darling, you must be patient. I know how much you feel you are missing out but I promise, by the time you are eighteen, I hope to have you awaiting surgery if that is still what you want.'

'It will be, it's all I ever wanted.'

'I know dear, it's very frustrating for you, but as I have read, a few turn back. I would not like that to be you and we would find it impossible to make you a whole boy again. If you are still convinced at eighteen, well, full steam ahead to ladyville.'

'Ladyville? Thanks mum.'

'Now think what you will wear tomorrow."

'I know already, the dress I wore for my birthday coming out and my glitzy sandals.'

'Wash your hair this evening. How do you want it?'

'Just straight mum and curled under. I just want it to grow so I can really do things with it.'

'Well wash tonight and I'll finish it off tomorrow.'

In the morning I'm all poshed up and the three of us drive to Brighton. We enter a house not far from the sea front, the posh, upmarket Hove end of the seafront. We sit in a waiting room that actually has nice up to date magazines and proper furniture.

A nurse calls Summer Somerville and we all rise.

'Just Summer please.' The nurse says and mum and Kayleigh sit and I go follow the nurse alone.

I enter a room that looks like a study and I'm pleased to see not a man behind the desk but a lady. She rises and holds out a hand and I shake hands and she introduces herself as Dr Jean Rose.

I sit and she asks questions. How long have I felt this way? Why is being a girl more attractive to me than being a boy?

I ask her if she would like to be a boy?

'I'm not trying to be a boy, I'm happy as a female.'

'I'm unhappy as a boy and I like being a girl and feel right as a girl. I have always felt like that, since I can remember. Life has been awful, a longing for what I was not and rejection of what I'm supposed to be. Since I started dressing as a girl and being treated as a girl, I feel so much happier.'

'I see from what your foster parent has said, your schoolwork started to improve as soon as you started living with them. At that time you were still outwardly a boy, going to school as a boy. Are you sure that your new found happiness is not just being in a nice family, rather than posing as a female?'

'It's true my work improved and yes, I was immediately happier when I started living with the Dawson's. Kayleigh has helped me with my work and explained things better than any teacher. But what really makes me happy is looking like, and being seen as a girl, treated as a girl and wearing girl clothes.'

'Why is it that wearing girl clothes makes you happy? Do you get a sexual thrill? Do you masturbate looking in the mirror?'

'No, I never have. I hate my male bits. I touch them as little as possible. Yes I do like my image when I'm

263

dressed as a girl, of course I do, like most girls like to see themselves looking smart and clean and attractive. Surely that isn't wrong? I mean girls practise expressions and poses in the mirror, so do I. I like to experiment with makeup, trying different things, but girls do that.'

'What about boys? Don't you relate to them at all.'

'I acted as a boy, I mean I played the part of being a boy because it was better than being beaten up and bullied. But I still tried to be smart and clean. I hated that act, pretending that I was a tough little nut. Oh yes my dad taught me to fight and I can, and a reputation as a fighter saved me from discovery as trans but also prevented the bullies from having a go, but all the time, I looked at the girls with envy. I wanted plaits, I wanted to wear the school uniform pleated skirt and the white blouse, tights in winter and girl shoes. I wanted to play their games. Convention made me act the boy because in school people like me are beaten up if our real character is discovered.'

'Yes but you plan to return to school as a girl. Have you considered you will be bullied?'

'Yes. It's a high price but one I have to pay. It's a stepping stone. I have a circle who I hope will support me, but there are always bullies.'

'Then you are determined, convinced that you must follow this path. Thank You Summer. Now would you mind if I brought in your Mum as you call her and your sister Kayleigh into our conversation? Then we will have a good talk together and I will explain some things and some rules.'

'Does that mean you will let me have oestrogen?'

'Let us have our talk, together and I will explain things.'

She rises from behind her desk. She offers a hand and takes mine. So we go into another room, the four of us. This room is informal, like a small sitting room with easy chairs and a coffee machine, one of those where you put little pouches in the top and out pops coffee, tea or chocolate from the bottom. We all select our drinks from a set of draws of different types of drink. It's real nice, homely and I'm much less frightened and on my guard. I was looking for a fight, to get my own way but this all seems so reasonable.

When we are all sat she says to mum and Kayleigh, 'How do you see Summer?'

'She is so a girl. Before, when he was Peter a boy in the class, he appeared a bit of a dunce, dull, like repressed and he had a reputation for being able to lash out and bash someone however big, but Peter was never a bully, in fact he would befriend those that were bullied. I always liked what I saw, I mean there was something about the boy I was attracted to, like the way he would flick his head to get his coif out of his face or I watched his hands, that in spite of being able to land a punch, were used more like a girl would use hands, with a delicate touch. Little hints in Peter's behaviour told me there was so much more below the surface of his projected manhood. I was fascinated and yet, I don't much like boys. I'm lesbian.'

'Well that is an interesting speech in so many ways. Rosalind, how do you see Summer?'

'When he first appeared, I just thought he was a rather quiet, quite well mannered young boy, actually immature for his age and very much so compared to my rather forward daughter. That they were friends and really liked each other was obvious. Kayleigh was almost a mother figure or an older sister, and she is nearly a year older. Peter was then shy, quite timid. There was no fear in my mind that anything was going on between them, under age sex for example and knowing my daughter's attitudes, I was satisfied that their relationship was platonic but already there was a deep bond there. I thought it was a natural mothering instinct with Kayleigh and deprivation on the part of Peter. So I arrived back after a night away and found these two together in bed. I was so shocked and cross. Then I found that Peter was also wearing a nightie, that they slept together because of needing comfort, like two sisters might, and that Peter was really Summer, that they were two girls in the bed.

Mum smiles and puts her arm out and caresses the back of my neck. She knows how I love that and I turn and smile too.

'She is so natural as a girl. She loves clothes and makeup. She is feminine, in fact sometimes more girl than Kayleigh, more frightened of trying something new. It is just her genitalia that defines her sex as male. I can understand in her position, in a children's home and at a school that contains a rough element as well as those from better homes, she had to maintain an image. The image is not her, just a disguise. I find it extraordinary that she could maintain it but then we all play parts in this world don't we, most of us offering a façade to the world that disguises the thoughts and attitudes within. I love Summer as though she was my own.'

'A happy family then. Your husband approves too?'

'Oh yes, Harry likes her immensely.'

'Well Summer as we will call you, do you see yourself as a girl?'

I hesitate, trying to order my thoughts and I'm very afraid I will say the wrong thing and my whole future will be undone.

'I want to be a girl. I'm not sure I am yet, I mean just putting on this dress and my lovely sandals and painting face and nails, doesn't make me a girl. I just feel a bit of a freak. I like what I see, I wish it were true, that image I see in the mirror looks like a girl but I know that underneath, I'm still boy as defined by genitalia. I hate what's down there. I hate it being seen. When doctor asked me to show her, I was so ashamed like a confession that I was a fraud. I always hated it. I mean boys play with theirs, their favourite toy, some in the home always had it out, boasting about size and things. I'm ashamed of having it.'

'So you don't feel normal?'

'No I don't. Not normal as a boy, nor as a girl but I'm a wanabee girl. I want that thing, those things gone. I want to have a vagina. I wish I could get pregnant and have a baby one day, but I probably never will. I wish I was not a freak.'

'You are not a freak Summer. Let me explain something. Sexuality and gender are not simultaneous in the womb. The brain, the Id that defines our sense of who we are and the genitalia develop at different times and can be affected by the chemical, hormonal balance of the mother, for example, she may have excess oestrogen or a flow of testosterone. Women don't make much testosterone compared to men but they do make some.'

I interrupt. 'I've read all that. I said that at my coming out birthday party.'

'Good but I better say it again. So genitalia and the development of the brain, take place at different speeds, and different stages in the foetus. They do not go hand in hand. The World is not divided into either or, male or female, you know that. Religions have taught throughout the social evolution of mankind, that sex and gender are the same, that a boy with a penis or girl with a clit are the perfect couple, a binary arrangement and the only one that exists. Governments too have clung to that idea. It makes life so simple, for example as in the toilet controversy in the United States, where some States have brought into law that people use the loo according to their birth gender. That would mean you today in your lovely dress and looking pretty and all girl, would be using a male toilet. How would that work? You would probably end up being assaulted sexually, beaten up or even killed. Religion has much to do with these attitudes and I'm afraid to say, practically all religions in the World are repressive. A dear friend of mine is a Church of England priest and insists the word marriage means the joining of a man and a woman. Does it I ask? Does it not just mean joining, like the marriage of ideas or two companies amalgamating, why does it have to be just male and female. 'Oh because the Bible says' they say. Who wrote the bible? Men who wanted to impart their ideas of this World and how humans should behave. They were relative to us, ignorant, they had no science, no understanding of chemistry or biology or the universe.

'Sexuality and gender are a continuum,' she continues.

'That's what I told Summer.' Kayleigh says.

'Good Kayleigh. In the cauldron of chemicals that whirl around in the womb and possibly before the womb, maybe in the man's sperm too, there is no one formula. All sorts of things happen that contribute to the child that finally emerges. Gestation is completely random, so many things may affect the foetus and when birth finally occurs, we count fingers and toes and rejoice if everything is in place, yet children are born with indefinite genitalia, or fingers missing or an extra digit or some other part missing. It is a lottery and even if the baby has all the right parts and looks and behaves normally, that is not the end of it because body and brain do not necessarily coincide, as in your case Summer. So normal, there is no normal. We are not coins stamped out at the Royal Mint, each one exactly like the last. We are all different, in talents, in appearance, in attitudes, in sexuality and in gender. If our outward appearance can vary so much, why would anyone expect our brains and sexual attitudes to be identical? They are as varied as our outward appearances. Some women love sex with a man, others with a woman, some don't like it at all, some find it bearable and go through the motions. Men are the same. Some people are cisgender, happy in their birth gender, some transgender or transsexual and hate their bodies and wish to transition. All these variations in human sexual orientation are normal but it is true to say that transsexuals are a minority. So do not think yourself abnormal more than the next. Just because others find it easy to live the binary way, boy and girl, doesn't make you wrong. We are what we are. There is no shame in being different, in fact I would say the reverse. Being trans as you call it is just another birth defect, the same as having webbed feet, but because it concerns that most important of human preoccupations, sex, much more emphasis is put on it. Being different in this human world that expects one to conform in one of two ways according to what is between the legs and rising above that and being a whole and decent person in whatever way one can, is something to be proud of, because you will have overcome a birth defect, a disadvantage. So be proud, look the World in the face and be happy Summer. Do you understand?'

'Yes doctor. Thank you.'

'Summer lastly I will say to you and you can say to others, only an ignorant fool would expect everyone in this World to conform to one sexual blue print or the other. Sex and gender are not a computer World, they are not binary, either or, Summer. You both understand that too mum and Kayleigh?'

They nod and smile and I think they get it and I do feel more normal and less ashamed.

'Very well. I would like to see you again in two months. I cannot by law give oestrogen or progesterone until you are sixteen, but I'm sure that this time next year I will prescribe drugs to make you feminine that will give you breasts and feminise your features even more and give you nice female skin and a figure more like a girl's. Then If you are still happy and stable, I will put you on the list for surgery and by early eighteen, you will be complete. Any questions from anyone?'

I just wanted to get out of there but I also wanted to hug every one. I got up and so did we all. 'Thank you doctor,' I say, 'you've been great and I do now feel proud.'

Outside I hug and kiss mum and Kayleigh and I cry a little with tears of joy, see I'm quite normally abnormal, not a sinner, not a freak, just a human.

Chapter 23.

Next week we return to school and of course I'm now Summer Somerville, in my little pleated skirt, four inches above my knee and wearing my clean, white short sleeve blouse and navy blazer, in tights and girl shoes with a one and a half inch heel, all we are allowed to get away with. I look in the mirror and think wow, here goes and I wonder how much I will be picked on. The thing is, kids are just people but many are just half civilised according to parents attitudes and some of them, rich as well as poor are just plain nasty. Anyway, I have about ten friends I can count on.

Immediately things start to happen for in class Mr Chapell our new form master in year eleven, reads out my name and of course a boy chortles and I know it's my old adversary Martin. He comes from a good family, his father owning a large farm in Surrey as well as a market garden South of Purley.

Chapell pulls up. He looks around the class and his eyes light upon Martin.

'Stand up Martin.'

Martin stands a grin on his face, a smile of bravado.

'Was someone telling a joke that made you laugh so indecorously Martin?' Chapell asks.

'Sir?'

'What don't you understand Martin? Is putting two or three words together too much for your juvenile brain?'

'Sir, no sir.'

'Then why did you imitate a hyena, boy?'

'Summer Somerville sir.'

'Oh I see, that was the joke, not about Summer herself? Only Martin can you see that laughing at a name is ignorance or laughing at anyone because they are different is not only ignorant but rude?'

'Sir, yes sir.' Martin says.

'Very well Martin. By assembly tomorrow I want a twenty line poem about Martin, from you, all the funny things that go with being Martin.'

'Sir there aren't any sir.'

'Oh but there are Martin, for example, you have one ear that sticks out more than the other and I have seen you playing rugby and you appear pin or pigeon toed. Was your mum or dad a pigeon?'

'No sir of course not.'

'A poem by tomorrow, to read to the class.'

'Sir.'

There were titters around the class.

So the rest of the register went on in silence. Afterwards as we filed out to our classes, Chapell asked me to stay. Kayleigh lingered at the door.

'Summer, I wonder whether it would be worth your explaining things to these immature brains. After all, what is happening with you is not usual is it, and beyond their experience. It might help knock some of this tomfoolery on the head and give you peace.'

'Yes sir I will sir.'

'Good girl and Summer, you look the part. Suits you Summer.'

'Thank you Mr Chapell.'

As I walked the corridor to catch up with the class, Martin appeared from behind the lockers. I'm glad Kayleigh had waited for me.

'You queer boy. You got me in it. I'm going to get you.'

'You got yourself in it Martin. Why do you always have to be so horrible?'

'Because I don't like you, never have and now I know why.'

'Oh Martin, grow up.' And I walk away.

Kayleigh laughs. 'Martin you really are an idiot.' She says.

He grabs my arm and books spill from my bag. There's a shout from behind. 'You boy, leave the girl alone. Come her at once.'

It's the new Deputy Head, Mr Carstairs. So I turn to go to Carstairs, thinking that he wants us both. 'No not you Summer, that boy Martin is it? Come here at once.'

I trot to the next class, history another of the classes that Kayleigh and I attend together. We have to sit apart being last in.

Miss Lawrence asks, 'Summer Somerville and Kayleigh, why are you late?'

'Had to see Mr Chapell miss and then the Deputy Head Mr Carstairs wanted a word.'

'Very well Summer but do be on time, we were waiting for you.'

'Yes miss.'

'And you are joined at the hip, the two of you?'

'No miss,' Kayleigh says. 'She's my sister Miss and we look out for each other.'

Miss looks at us both sternly, then smiles. 'Commendable. Just be on time.'

Next we do geography, again together and this time we sit together. And then it's morning break for fifteen minutes. Martin and his two sidekicks walk by. He leers and smiles. 'I will get you. Wearing panties won't save you.'

'Oh do grow up Martin,' I say. 'One day you will have to run your dad's business and you will have to deal with all sorts of people. They will not necessarily be the people you like but they have a right to be whomever they are so just leave me alone. I thrashed you once before and I can still thrash you, but it will be even worse for your reputation next time because I'm wearing a skirt. Think whether you want to chance that.'

He is red in the face, puce I think they say in books and his two henchmen smile which I think must also annoy him. He has lost face as the Chinese say.

However over the next few days, a lot of pettiness goes on, remarks and lewd sketches left on the white boards and my locker has pervert scrawled on it in different colours. The final straw is when I walk into assembly and Mr Chapell arrives behind me. On the board in bold letters is; 'A faggot by any other name would stink as bad,' parodying Shakespeare's 'A rose by any other name would smell as sweet.'

Chapell is furious. 'Who wrote this?' he demands, his face is almost luminous with anger. The class that had been rumbling with sniggers and whispers falls deathly quiet. 'Come on, own up or the whole class will be in detention for half an hour each day for a week, bar Summer and Kayleigh.'

There are immediate protests from everyone; that they will miss buses or a violin class; another says they have tennis coaching and another that their sister is home from America and they are having a family meal.

'Right,' Chapell says, 'I will distribute ballot forms and you will all write anonymously who did it. You understand anonymously?'

'Sir, it's not fair sir.' Danny Chase says, always a wimp.

'And why not Daniel?'

'Because sir the thugs could say it was an innocent person.'

'They could. Therefore we need all the good people to write the correct culprit, because like a ballot, the person who receives the most votes will be guilty.'

So there is a lot of shifting in seats and arms curled around the slips of paper so prying eyes cannot see. Others like Martin and his two henchman Andrew Little and Tim Tetherby are peering around, trying to see who is writing what.

Chapell says, 'You three, Martin, Tetherby and Little. Wait outside.'

'But we want to vote to sir.' Martin wails.

'And you shall Martin, when I allow you back in. You have extra time to write a name or admit guilt.'

So I see some writing, others just scribbling. The slips are folded and Chapell collects them in the waste bin.

We all sit while he divides them into three piles. He then admits Martin and company who present theirs.

'Interesting Martin. You say it was Summer that wrote that to get you into trouble and your friends say the same. Summer, did you put that on the board?'

'No sir.'

'I thought not. I have seven spoiled papers, five saying it was Shakespeare, two for Tony Blair and this largest pile say Martin. Robert Martin, to save the form from detention all week, did you do this? Own up Martin or face the consequences.'

'It's not fair sir. He must be a faggot.'

'I'll take that as an admission Martin. Off you go and sit in the hall. I shall speak to Mr Grainger.'

'Fucking pervert.' Martin yells as he leaves the room.

That's the last I see of Martin. He never returns to school so presumably as a reward, his dad has paid fees for him at a private school.

I'm glad my chief taunter and school long adversary has gone. A spoiled child with too much money and little discipline had made him a bully.

Chapter 24.

As Chapell suggested I give my speech to the class. I'm even more nervous amongst these kids than at my party.

'You have all known me first as Peter Wallace the loner, the little thug and now as well, who and what I am now, Summer. When I was Peter, I acted tough so people would leave me alone. If they left me alone, I thought they wouldn't discover who I really was, a girl with the wrong body, a boy body with a girl brain. I know that's really difficult for you to understand because you have grown up as who you are, boys in boy bodies and girls in girl bodies and happy to be so. That's called cisgender, happy in your own body. I am transgender or transsexual. I have gender dysphoria. Dysphoria is a Greek word meaning discontent, an unease, unhappiness. So unhappiness with my gender, being a boy. Every minute of every day I felt wrong in my boy body, that it should not belong to me. I knew I ought to have a girl body and girl clothes and to be regarded as a girl by others and have all the things a girl has that a boy does not because my girl brain was telling me that. There are a lot of girls too that want to have boy bodies. Because it is now possible, I shall go all the way to make my body female, with breasts and a clitoris and vagina.' There are a few sniggers and Chapell looks annoyed. 'Then I will be happy enough to go on living. In the past, up to fifty per cent who felt as I do, committed suicide because they were unhappy. The suicide rate in those who have transitioned is around, even a bit below that of the average. The main cause of suicide in trans people is bullying by the so called normal. I shan't have babies because I haven't a womb or ovaries, but I shall be a girl apart from that and there are girls born every week that have some essential girl bits missing, ovaries for example and many girls find they cannot reproduce. That doesn't make them boys, just that they are girls with bits missing.

'Why you want to ask, do I want to be a girl? Because then my body will be as near as possible to what my brain tells me to be and instead of my brain being at war with my body, my brain will be content. Every one of us is different, so there is no normal. The trouble is the human animal is too intelligent. Other animals we believe are pleased to just be, your cat catching mice and birds, a deer grazing. Humans want to know everything and when we don't know, we make up theories, like at one time, the World was flat and if you sailed far enough you would fall off the edge. They found the World was round and they found we were not made of clay in the Garden of Eden. We evolved from tiny microbes in the sea. At the time of the dinosaurs, we didn't exist in anywhere near human form.

'God did not make us out of clay as people once believed and as was written in the scriptures. Those writings were by men who tried to understand, as most of us do, why we are here on this little Earth that is filling up with people. We now know there was no garden of Eden, or Adam and then Eve created by God. According to the Scriptures, that's the writings of men who in their time were wise but by today's standards ignorant and superstitious. God made us in his own image, the Scriptures say, but we now know that is also false unless he was a large creepy crawly. The World was not made in six days and on the sixth God rested, was another myth. That film 10,000 years BC where a pterodactyl carries off a woman was just nonsense. The dinosaurs were only seventy five million years ago, but the World is at least five billion years old. So all that Old Testament stuff about Eden and Noah was just rubbish, men trying to make sense of it all and most of the Scriptures are folk tales.

'We have all those things in the Bible laying down rules. The ten commandments, said to be written on stone. They are good rules and are the basis of our laws. Then we have a lot more rules about not eating animals with a cloven hoof and they really meant pigs. Pig meat decays quickly in hot climates, the places where those rules were developed were hot. Even sixty years ago my granny tells me, you only ate pork and shell fish if there was a R in the month, so that meant not May, June, July or August, because they were the hot months. We all have refrigerators now so we can eat food like pig or shell fish at any time. Yet some people still abide by those old rules of the Bible. In a book called 'A Strange Life' the auto biography of a trans person, the authors doctor quoted the Bible as a reason why someone should not change sex.

There are one or two quotations that people like her doctor resorted to 'Genesis 1:27, which says, "So God created man in his own image, in the image of God he created him; male and female he created them.' I think we already dealt with that one. Deuteronomy 22:5, which says, 'A woman must not wear men's clothing, nor a man wear women's clothing, for the Lord your God detests anyone who does this.' We don't know when God actually said that. Dueteronomy was said to be written by Moses but was everything written actually inspired by God? Why is it that God does not send us new prophets? Where those old testament prophets and people like St Paul, just the wisest men in their time, in times of ignorance, who wrote down their theories as law. Genesis 1:27 says: "So God created mankind in his own image, in the image of God he created them; male and female he created them. That does not mean that he only created male and female, it is not necessarily a binary thing, but male and female are the poles of a continuum and includes all those variations in between.

'Should her doctor have used his religion to deny her treatment or should he have only used medical science in his judgement? Should the doctor have put aside his personal belief and have done what would make the patient a whole person? What would Jesus have done? I believe that Jesus was first and foremost a humanist, a humane person and would have looked after the patient.

'My doctor said this; 'People are so varied on the outside, I mean just English white people, some tall, some thin, some fat some small, some pretty and some not good looking. Others are born with a handicap, blind, deaf, an extra finger or with a mental handicap. Then there are all the other races that have just as many variations, yellow, brown, black and pink, so why do we presume that everyone should be sexually the same, girls liking boys and boys liking girls, hetero sexual and cisgender. That's as the Scriptures wanted us to be, but it's not so. Practically every family has someone gay in it, an uncle, aunt, sister brother or cousin. They used to be imprisoned for being gay, even killed fifty years ago. I'm a bit more rare, about one in ten to fifteen thousand are trans. But if anyone points at anyone of you and says, 'You are not normal, you should ask what is normal? It doesn't exist.'

'Thank you Summer. 'That's been really interesting and of course has been Summer's own views and opinions. We are all entitled to our own beliefs don't you think Summer?'

'Yes sir, but not the beliefs handed down by family, that's just indoctrination. Everyone should think things through and decide what they believe.'

'I'm sure that has made us all think and accept people who are more different than we like to think is normal. Well done Summer, a round of applause I think.'

They clap. My lovely Kayleigh says, 'Well done.' I blush.

'I don't know how I did that or where it all came from. I mean I had thought about it, but hadn't written it out properly.'

'It came from the heart of a really clever girl.' My lover says.

Afterwards a few kids come and say that was really interesting. One asks if I believe in God? She wears a Christian badge on her uniform. I look at her, look straight into her eyes. 'That's a big subject for the dinner queue.' I say, giving myself thinking time.'

'Well do you?'

'I believe in big bang, a huge explosion in space that flung gases billions of light years all over and then strange things happened where conditions were right for life as we know it to begin, for example vegetation, water, prime evil swamps from whence came creatures, eventually land creatures, then the dinosaurs and then a catastrophe and they died, then mammals, sabre toothed tigers, mammoths, huge bears and others and man developing from primitive creatures that crawled from the swamps and became apes and gradually mankind developed and is still developing. You want to know whether I believe in a nice old Grandpa sitting on a throne surrounded by angels, who looks down and can see and read the thoughts of everyone of us. You want to know whether I pray, for example, for war to end and for my mum to get better? I don't believe praying ever succeeded in deliverance from anything, a war, a plague, or famine or from a terrible car crash or for a baby to be born with all its right parts. So no to the sort of God you believe in. What I do believe is, when you make a decision, you could do worse and ask, 'What would Jesus do?' That should give you wise judgement.'

'Thank you Summer.' She turns away a frown on her face. I wonder if I have made her think rather than blindly following the faith she has been raised to believe.

She turns back. I think she may be annoyed or aggressive. Instead she says, 'How do you know all this stuff?'

'Because I was trying to make sense of myself, so I have read and read, philosophers, science, psychology and distilled it down to make my own judgements. It's far harder being an atheist than a believer. I just have myself as a prop, myself to blame.'

The remarks on the whiteboards stop and the janitor repaints the lockers and the bullying stops. Oh occasionally someone will shout a remark from a crowd, but often too, others will hiss at them to be quiet. By half term, things have settled down. I have my little clique and Kayleigh and I are invited to the same parties.

Mum is better than she has been. I dress in girl jeans and a nice top, a pink short sleeve blouse and girl flats. I tie my quite long hair back. Kayleigh appears.

'Mum's driving us.' she says.

'You're coming too?'

'I think it's time I met your mum, don't you?'

I think for a moment. 'OK, if you want. It's not always very nice.'

'Of course it isn't, but if we are to remain as a couple, then I have to don't I?'

'You don't have to.'

'I want to. I will support you no matter what. That's what love is. You would do the same for me, I know and perhaps, if your mum is seeing the girl for the first time, then you need extra support and I will be there to back you up.'

I look into her chestnut eyes as though they are a window into her brain. I kiss her on the lips. 'Thank you. I'm so lucky to have found you.'

'Found me?' she says indignantly, 'Who found who, mooching alone in the Mall, up to no good, I'll be bound?'

'You found me and I shall always love you for it and for everything you have given me.'

'Good. I want you to love me as I love you. I want in time to investigate your girl anatomy when that arrives.'

'You speak as though it's mail order.' I say.

'If only we could order up a new body on Amazon, with three hundred pages of bodies to choose from.' She says.

'I think that would make life just too complicated.' I say.

'Oh Summer, you are losing your sense of fun. You mustn't become a boring old lawyer. I want you to become a brilliant lawyer but with a sense of humour.'

'I shall remember that. You will be like Richard Branson, and abseil down a building in a ladies wedding dress will you?'

'Top hat and tails. Just remember he was a man. I'm a girl and pleased to be so.'

'I have no doubt of that.'

So we go to the hospital and we find mum in the Conservatory where she sits doing nothing, just looking at the gardens.

'Mum,' I say.

289

She turns and looks and smiles. 'Hello dear, I hoped you would come.'

'Did you mum? You sound brighter.'

'Yes dear I feel better. I think I'm sorting my head out.' She looks at Kayleigh. 'Are you a new nurse?'

'No mum, this is Kayleigh, I live with her now.'

'That's nice. Are you happy?'

'Yes mum. Mum look at me, look at what I'm wearing.'

'You look like a girl, your long hair and that top.'

'Mum, I need to tell you. I live as a girl mum, with Kayleigh and her mum and dad. I'm going to be a girl mum.'

'Well you look like a girl. You need to be careful people will get the wrong idea. It could get you into trouble.'

'Mum I'm changing sex mum, I live as a girl. I have changed my name to Summer Somerville, your name mum, a girl's name.'

'You're going to be a girl?'

'Yes mum. I'm going to be who I always wanted to be always believed I should be. I'm working hard too mum.

I want to go to university and become a lawyer. What do you think mum?'

'You're going to be a girl. Then you won't grow up to be like your dad? He turned out to be a wrong one, your dad. So you won't be like him?'

'No mum. I want to be a lawyer, helping poor people.'

'Is this your influence?' She has turned to Kayleigh.

'No Mrs Somerville. This is her, her real self. I just help her because I like and love her.'

I quickly step in. 'Mum I have always known I should be a girl. You remember I used to dress up a lot and play with your makeup.'

'Oh you were funny when you were a child and then he started teaching you how to hurt and I thought you would be just like him.'

'I won't be. I never want to see him again. I wish you could get better. Won't you try for me, try to get better.'

'I'm comfy here. I don't have to think. You say you are going to be a girl? How's that possible?'

'Medicine mum.' I hesitate to say surgery. That might be too much.

'Oh medicine. That's what they give me, medicine and look at me, no good for anything, and I look so old.'

'We all grow old mum. If you had a bit of makeup and a new hairdo, you would look beautiful again. When you come out of here, I'll take you somewhere and they will give you the works, hair and makeup, new clothes. You'd be like a new person. Wouldn't that be exciting.'

'You don't say much,' she says to Kayleigh. 'You just listen to this one chatter on making out life is so simple. It isn't. It's a disappointment, that's what it is.'

'Mum don't say that.'

'You look like a girl. Don't get a man, oh they tell you things, promises but they ruin you. I'm a bit tired now. I want a nap. A girl you say, well I suppose you can be a girl called Peter.'

'No mum, I have a new name. Summer and your maiden name, Somerville, nothing to do with Wallace.'

'Very nice dear. I always knew there was something, hoped you wouldn't turn out like your dad.'

'No fear of that. I wish you would get better. I need my mum.'

'Well they do say, I'm on the mend Peter. You need to change that to Petra. Thank you for coming and for bringing your friend. She looks nice.'

'She is mummy.'

'Mummy. You haven't called me that in years. You've changed. You're softer, but stay strong, not like me, weak. Have you seen my mum and dad?'

'No mum. They didn't want us did they, because of dad.'

'Speak to them dear, perhaps they will help you. Now I'm tired. Say goodbye. Kiss me dear.'

I kiss her. 'I'll come back soon mum. Glad to see you are feeling better.'

'Oh much better and better for seeing you too. I love you dear. I know I don't show it, forgotten how. You look a nice girl. Clean, sweet.'

'Bye mum.'

'Bye dear, bye to your friend.'

I kiss mum and we go and there's a great lump in my throat and I have held back the tears that now pour down my cheeks. Kayleigh rescues me with a tissue.

'That's so hard for you.'

'Terrible. I hate leaving her, like desertion, but what can I do. Still she was as good as I've seen her for a couple of years.'

I stop at the Matron's office. I knock the door and hear 'come in'.

'Oh do I know you.' Matron asks.

'I used to be Peter Wallace. I'm now called Summer Somerville. I've been seeing mum, Libby Wallace.'

'Oh. Well you do look nice. Did she understand who you were?'

'Oh yes.'

'How do you think she is?'

'She seemed a bit more in this World.'

'We have reduced her drugs and hope she will go on making progress. There's always a danger that reducing the drugs may be detrimental and we will have to revert but she seems at last to be facing the real World. She was all right with you?'

'Yes, not quite with it but better than she has been.'

'Summer we can't promise anything in a case like hers, but we would hope that in a year possibly, you might have mum back.'

Kayleigh holds my arm as we walk to the car. Mum Ros sit's on the lawn talking to someone. She sees us and we wait for her to join us.

'Well how was it?' She asks.

'Horrible,' I say.

Chapter 24.

I phone Granny Somerville.

'Hello, Mrs Somerville, speaking.'

'Granny. It's Peter, your grandson.'

'Well this is a surprise. After all these years. What do you want? Money?'

'Granny, I just need to see you. To talk. Granny none of the estrangement was my fault. I need to tell you things and then perhaps we can start over.'

'What things Peter?' Her tone has changed. The aggression gone, but suspicion is still there and I can't be surprised at that.

'An awful lot has changed Granny and I don't want to say it on the phone. I would really love to see you and tell you things and then you can make up your mind whether you would want to be my Gran or not.'

'I have missed you. It has been hard for me, for us. Grandad isn't well. He has been talking and talking about finding you.'

'Well then? Gran can I come and see you? Then if you want me as family, I can tell you about mum. She's not been well.'

'We know that. We tried to visit, but she refused to see us.'

'I need to see you.'

'Where are you?'

'I live with a nice family in Purley.'

'Do you? That's not too far. I would come there but your Grandpa, he doesn't travel far or travel well.'

'I could ask my foster mum to bring me over and my foster sister too, if that would be OK.'

'When dear?" I like the sound of her calling me dear. I haven't had that from her in years after they cut us off because mum had married dad. Their judgement of him had been right but cutting a child off, that is a hard judgement. In mum's case I think they had been wrong. It wasn't she that was bad.

'Perhaps Sunday if you are free.'

'Oh we're free. About four for afternoon tea and I'll bake.'

'Thanks Gran. There's something I need to tell you first. I'm now called Summer.'

'Summer? But that's one of those girl's modern names! How do you mean?'

'Yes Gran, I live as a girl now.'

There's a long silence. I wonder whether she has put the phone down.

'Gran?' I say, tremulously.

'We will expect you at four on Sunday.'

'Thanks Gran.'

I find Ros in the kitchen. 'Mum are we doing anything on Sunday?'

'No but I suspect we are now.'

'May we go to Sussex, to see my grandparents please? I haven't seen them but once in my life because they judged that mum had married a bad person. When I last saw them I think I was four. I phoned and Grandad isn't well but mum says Sunday tea would be fine, for us all.'

'And do they know just who is coming?'

'Well the three of us.'

'Yes but are they expecting three ladies or two ladies and a young man?'

'Oh three ladies.'

'Then we'll go. If you had said two ladies and a young man, I would have refused. So that's it, no more boy?'

'That's it mum. No more Peter. Tell the truth and shame the devil.'

'Good girl. Wear something pretty and don't be afraid to be a girl.'

'No mum, I'm not afraid any more.'

Sunday arrives and I am dreading it yet excited. My grandparents were always like figures of mythology to me, never spoken of by dad, well he had none that I knew of although of course he must have had them and mums were denigrated by dad and tearfully remembered by mum. I can't even remember what they look like.

Mum Ros comes home from her Saturday in London at eleven Sunday morning as usual from seeing delightful Davina and Kayleigh and I are ready to go out to lunch as arranged. I'm wearing a lovely day dress in a semi transparent blue flowered material that has an under skirt sewn in. I bought it in Wallis in a mad moment for more money than I should but I'm not sorry. We are eating at a place in Sussex a county in Southern England that has everything to my mind, sea shore, the South Downs, very expensive houses and old farm houses and sheep still on the hills that keep the grass close cropped and it's good for walkers. A lot of rich people live there.

The pub we stop at has a large car park and the cars range from the tiny Smart car to a Bentley and even a Maserati as well as more normal makes like Ford and VW. The building itself is old red brick, the hand crafted ones and the walls are adorned with vines and climbers that hang over some windows.

The inside is carpeted throughout apart from the public bar. The public bar in England is where local people go to drink, pints of ale[9] in particular, but these days when gin has become a fashionable drink again mum says, all sorts of bespoke gins, a variation on a theme by adding what she calls botanicals, various different herbs.

Local people sometimes have their own mugs hanging up and in this case as we walk through, I see old blackened beams, quarry tiles on the floor that range in colour from deep red to almost cream and dark oak furniture. There are several beer pumps lining the bar bearing the names of unknown local breweries that are often just a two man affair each making beer in the ancient manner using real hops and malted barley or whatever else they put in.

None of that is for us. We enter the lounge and find room to sit and a waiter takes our name and confirms our booking and hands the menus to us. We study things that are in French, an absolute annoyance to mum that she calls snobby nonsense, airs and graces. Just calling a dish by a French name doesn't make it good she says. What especially annoys is that some of the French is misspelt

[9] Ale, bitter beer a mainly light coloured of locally brewed beer that comes in a vast range from bespoke brewers.

and has accents and things missing as well as le for la and vice versa.

So we study and Mum Ros used to eating out with Davina in London, knows a thing or two about food. She interrogates the young waiter and he doesn't know anything. He runs off to ask. He is replaced by a young woman, darkly attractive who seems to know everything and possesses a lovely accent too. She is from Italy we find after mum interrogates her. I look and I'm fascinated by this young woman and think if only I was that attractive. She's like a bird, a bird face, sharply defined features but placed in a nice symmetrical pattern and her smile and her serious thinking expressions are beautiful. Her hands are as slim as her figure and her hips are rounded. Her lace edged apron sits flat upon her tummy, her skirt is wow high and slim legs shod in black patent with a two inch heal.

We choose, chicken for me, lamb for mum and fish for Kayleigh. When the girl has gone, I say, 'I wish I could look like her.'

Mum says, 'Bless you girl, you do, not a carbon copy but you are as attractive and becoming more so. I see such a difference since you first entered our house as a shy boy.'

Kayleigh squeezes my hand. 'Mum's right, you could be that girl's sister only you are blonde, really. Be confident you are an attractive young lady.'

I'm pleased and embarrassed and half believe what they say, but wonder if they just praise to boost me. I continually scan my reflection, hoping that any sign of boy is absent, only half believing that I really do look like a girl and not a macabre trannie.

The Italian girl returns and we are shown to our table. It is proper dining, white damask table cloth and serviettes, sparking glasses and clean silverware. The boy waiter we first saw and who knew nothing, assists us to sit and I feel such a fraud. He actually smiles at me and as he hands me the serviette, his hand touches mine. I receive a jolt like an electric shock.

When he's gone, Kayleigh says with a smile, 'He was flirting with you Summer.'

'He wasn't.' I say.

'I think he was,' Mum says. 'Summer, you may not see it, and I would not call you beautiful, but you are attractive. There is something about your features that is almost magnetic, one wants to touch just as one wishes to touch a fascinating sculpture.'

Although these two are my family, I blush. I wonder whether it's true? Is it just me and my self-consciousness that can still see Peter. Do I really look like Summer? I hope so. I hope I pass.

A bottle of pink wine appears and we are having a glass, the first time I have ever had wine. It's a lovely pink, quite subtle and when poured in the glass effervesces, tiny bubbles clinging to the sides and others floating to the surface.

We have starters and then mains and as the portions are tiny, manage a sweet too. We take coffee in the large lounge that has views of the Downs, grass hills with the occasional farm house, clumps of woodland that on this sunny autumn day look just lovely in their pre winter colours.

'Now Summer, be confident with gran and granddad. Be loving if that is how you feel, after all you asked for this meeting and they expect a girl and so be a girl. Don't go into your shell and put on the boy. I've seen you do that as though you are ashamed of how you are. You want to be a girl and are happy as a girl, so be one.'

We sit and have coffee and the place is still busy, even at three thirty as walkers and others come in for a late lunch and somehow the place keeps serving good food.

We make our way to the car and have a few miles to reach the Gramps. I just don't know what to expect. We find Amberley is a village on the north side of the downs, in a hollow and protected from the sea gales. We find the address and discover a typical old Sussex house with half tiled exterior walls and a sagging clay tiled roof that is moss covered. The front door is black oak but the window frames are fresh white paint and the front garden possesses a circular drive. It must be worth a fortune in these days.

We ring the bell and stand and Ros has pushed me forward. The door opens and there stands Granny. I can see mum in her.

'Hi Granny, I'm Summer.'

She just looks and I wonder if this is going to be a disaster and the door will slam in my face.

'I know you are. I can see my daughter in you, as she was at your age. You so look like her, it took my breath away.' She kisses my forehead and then both cheeks and takes my hand and draws me in.

We all enter and I introduce Ros and Kayleigh in the ample hallway. A grandfather clock strikes four and a faint memory of this house stirs. I have been here before, years ago so the memory is like a dream.

'Come into the kitchen. Grandfather is in the lounge having a nap, so we won't disturb him yet, and I can get to know you all and I can catch up on what has happened.'

So we drink tea and lemonade, the clear sort that tastes like no lemon I ever tasted but it is nice all the same.

I answer so many questions, especially about my rogue father and then mum's illness.

There are suddenly tears in Grans eyes and so then in mine and we both stand and cry and it's so beautiful. 'Grannie,' I say.

'Summer, I'm so pleased to see you. Now you have to tell me all about yourself and being a girl.'

So I tell all, explaining as best I can in as few words as possible and Kayleigh sometimes backs me when she feels she can and Mum Ros holds my hand. Gran speaks to them both and they are so kind in their words and judgements of me. Gran gets up and brings out cakes and cups and a great white teapot. The door opens and Grandpa stands in the doorway. He is small as though he has deflated and is now only just taller than Gran. He still has hair, silver and with a parting. His skin is smooth and pink and white and drawn.

'I thought I heard voices. Why did you leave me out of this reunion Jane?'

'I thought best to let you sleep dear.'

'Well I wasn't asleep and I saw the car outside so realised our visitors had arrived. So who is my grand daughter?'

'It's me grandfather,' I say, rather in awe.

'Then I demand a kiss and a cuddle. I've missed you.' I see a tear in his eye and his lower lids fall away from his eyes.

He kisses on the lips and holds me tight. 'I wish I had seen you grow up. Summer, it's a funny name but then this is a peculiar age. However, a rose by any other name would smell as sweet and it's sweet to have you here and meet after all these years.'

We sit again and I introduce Kayleigh and Ros and we eat cake and I tell my history. We go into the lounge and the lights go on and the curtains are drawn as darkness has fallen and still we sit and talk. They are interested in my future and say they would have me there but that they understand it is better for Kayleigh and I to be together and there is school to consider.

'Would your mother come to us?' Gran asks. 'Get her out of the clutches of those doctors? I feel she might do better here?'

'I don't know Granny. She is so up and down, so dependent on the drugs they pump into her.'

'I'd like her to come home Jane.' Grandpa says.

'Yes you would and so would I but you know who would do all the work of nursing you both. We'll see. I will speak to the hospital and if she will see me, speak to her. It won't be easy.'

We leave at nine in the evening, promising to come again soon and I also promise to phone once a week. It's kisses all around and lots of tears. I'm quite overcome and hardly talk all the way home.

'Mum,' I say, 'thank you for today. It has been absolutely brill and I so love you for giving it me.'

Kayleigh says, 'You are such a lovely sloppy girl, Summer. It's been a good day for us too hasn't it mum? Making you happy Summer makes us happy.'

Chapter 25.

A week later as we do homework, I hear the doorbell go and voices in the hall and then footsteps on the stairs. The bedroom door opens and Ros says quietly, 'Leave what you're doing and come down please.'

We go down, mystified and I think Grandpa has died. The idea shoots into my brain and I'm already half in tears.

We go into the lounge and a man stands there that I have never seen before and a female officer in uniform sits on the other settee. I think what's going on? Taking a lead from mum, Kayleigh and I seat ourselves on the three seat settee and this stranger in a dark suit says, 'I'm Detective Sergeant Andrews. I've come from St Cecilia's Psychiatric Hospital. I have to inform you Summer, that your mother has died. I'm sorry to bring such sad news.'

There's complete silence. I try to take in, process the words. Kayleigh's hand has reached for mine and has tightened around it.

'How? She was so much better.' I say.

'We can't say yet. There will have to be an autopsy and an inquest, but we suspect a drugs overdose. Somehow she had got hold of a substantial amount and swallowed most of them, more than enough to kill herself we believe, but it's not proven yet. If so it was deliberate.

We have to find out how she obtained them. I'm sorry to bring such appalling news.'

'But she was in a hospital. She was getting better.'

'That's what everyone thought. You may not know, but she has made an attempt several times according to their records. That's why you have been advised not to visit from time to time. You were her only visitor Summer. She left a note which you may read, but we have to keep it as evidence. Do you wish to read it?'

'I had better.'

He passes a photocopy. I would have liked the real thing, the one mum must have slaved over. I read it.

Dearest Summer, I'm so happy you have found yourself and you are with a good family who can give you everything I cannot. I'm sorry I have been such a poor apology for a mother and that you have struggled alone.

'You are such a pretty and clever girl, I know you will go on to do great things and I saw the love between you and your Kayleigh. Cherish and love each other and keep a small place in your heart for memories of me when things were better. I remember especially our last holiday, in Wales at the Old Coastguard Cottage when we went off on our own adventures and the ice creams and paddling in the rock pools.

I thought then how like a girl you were and how like I was at that age, a tomboy. If only I had been more feminine, I don't think I would have been a rebel and fallen for your dad and life would have been so different, but then too he and I would not have made you. You are worth everything, all the pain, all the shouting and all the love. God bless you Summer, do well for me. I love you. Mum xxx

I sink back into the settee. I can't understand how that can be. I'm so angry.

'How? They were supposed to look after her not kill her.' I say.

'That's what we will be investigating. How she obtained enough drugs to commit suicide. We are sorry to bring such bad news. You are living here permanently miss?'

I make no reply. I'm still trying to process this information.

'Yes she is.' Ros says.

'According to our information, you saw your mother just six days ago. We will come back for a statement about your visit and mum's state of mind then. Was anyone with you?'

'Yes my foster mother drove me there but stayed outside in the garden but my foster sister came with me to see mum.'

'Thank you. We will come back and take a statement about your visit from you both when you have had time to assimilate this news.'

'Why not now? We are both here. The visit is fresh in my mind. Do it now and get it out of the way. Please.' I say feeling strong maybe from the anger I feel towards the hospital.

'Are you sure Miss?'

'Yes, dammit. I don't want a visit from you hanging over me.'

'Then we better take a statement from you both separately.'

It's the female copper who sits with me in the kitchen, taking my statement while the Sergeant goes back to the car. I'm glad it's the woman. She's business-like but kind. I tell her as near as verbatim, I think that's the word, as I remember, including my visit to Matron.

Then it is Kayleigh's turn to be in the kitchen. After nearly an hour and a half, they depart.

Somehow I feel OK. 'What are we doing for dinner?' I ask.

'You needn't worry about that Summer.'

'I want something to do?'

'Your homework, both of you. I'll do dinner. Are you sure you can eat dinner Summer?'

'Of course, why not?' I say indignantly snapping at mum.

'Up you go and do homework. I'll call when dinner's ready, both of you.'

I see a look pass between mum and Kayleigh, conspiratorial and I know they think I'm barking.

'Oh sod it all.' I say and make for the stairs. Half way up I falter, stumble and I feel ill. I make it to the loo and empty my stomach and then keep retching.

Kayleigh comes in and watches me and holds my head, her hand across my forehead. She helps me up and then I start bawling. She wipes my face with cotton pads and pours me a glass of water I sip and sip and sit on the side of the bath, rocking back and forth.

'Come along Summ, I'm getting you into bed. No school for you tomorrow.'

She leads me to her room and strips me down and puts on my nightie and tucks me in. She hands me a pill and a glass of water and I swallow the pill without asking what it is. She kisses my cheek.

'Go to sleep. I shall be here and later I'll come to bed.'

I start to cry, for mum and in anger that they allowed her to die in care and I cry because Kayleigh and Ros are just so giving. I cry because I have seen the Gramps and I thought we would all get on a level again and now this. I cry because I'm angry that mum hoodwinked us all into believing she was on the mend yet she must have planned this, stored up tablets unless she had access to the drugs cabinet. I fall asleep.

I don't hear Kayleigh come to bed, don't even feel her. I wake in the morning and I'm alone. I look at my watch. It's nine o'clock. I should be at school. I jump out of bed and run to the loo. When I return to the bedroom, I find Mum Ros there.

'I'm late.' I say.

'You are at home with me today, perhaps the rest of the week Summer. Into bed or do you want to get dressed and we'll go for a walk?'

'I'll get up mum.'

'Make yourself look nice Summer.'

So I get washed and dressed. I look in the mirror and see Peter and I hate myself. I wonder whether I'm the reason mum committed suicide. I hope not. I do my face, eyebrows, lashes and eyeliner.

I find breakfast is all ready for me. Normally I would get it myself but mum has prepared porridge and fruit so I am more or less compelled to eat. She must have known that left to my own devices I wouldn't have bothered. Somehow I force it down but I'm fighting nausea.

I can't face tea and I have a glass of water that I just sip.

'Let me look at you Summer.' She peers at me and then does that thing all mums do, feels my forehead. She kisses me on the lips, the first time she has done that and I break down. The tears that have been absent, flow and I sob uncontrollably. 'Mum' I keep saying the word and Ros hugs me hard and won't let me go and covers my forehead with kisses and strokes my hair. I don't know how long I howl, but mum allows me to, encourages me to, saying, 'That's right, let it all out Summer, howl as loudly as you like. You need to do this.'

Gradually my howl falls into sobs and then gulps for breath. Mum dries my eyes and dabs my cheeks.

'You need to repair that makeup. Then we'll go out. We'll have lunch out.'

'I wish Kayleigh was with us mum.'

'I should have thought of that. I'll text her.'

Minutes later, we receive a text back. 'We'll pick her up at the school gate, so as soon as you're ready.'

We pick Sis up at the gate and she changes into Jeans and a sloppy jumper as we drive. We go to Dorking and then to the foot of Boxhill. We park at Ryka's Café and take the footpath to the top.

It's a good late autumn day. The sun has arrived late and the clouds cleared and blue skies stretch for ever with just a line, a cloud bank far to the south. It's a long steep haul and the zig-zag road that takes traffic up, formed part of the 2012 Olympics cycle route. At the top we walk the beach forest, shuffling in the leaves and we all, mum included, have a leaf fight. We brush ourselves down and pick leaves from each other's hair in mutual grooming. Afterwards we walk back down and have burgers and chips at the café. From there we drive into Epsom and go to the cinema. We see Miss Sloane, the only film we fancy but we find it thrilling.

We are home by eight. Mum picks the post off the mat and looks through it. Six of the eight envelopes are just rubbish and go straight in the bin. The seventh is from her mum in Scotland, I have yet to meet her.

The last contains a thick wodge of papers. 'Summer,' Mum says. 'These are your adoption papers. I would like you to read them and then make your mind up whether you want to be a permanent member of our family.'

'Mum. Thank you. It's such a compliment. Whatever I decide, if it's no, it won't be because I don't want to. I love you and I love this family because there is so much love here even though you and Harry lead separate lives. I love being here and I love you all. I'm so lucky that Kayleigh saw something in me and brought me into the family. At the moment everything is too raw, too new and I'm in shock from mum's death I just want you to know, you guys are the best. I'm so lucky.'

Over the next days and weeks we hug a lot. I cry from time to time. The days when I was a boy and never cried are far behind me. I am no longer repressed, unable to relate to anyone. I still defend the ones at school who are targeted by bullies and I am bullied to an extent myself.

Some parents have made protests about me. That I use the girls' loos is the main complaint. Those people would fit right in with the red necks of Alabama, Arkansas, Illinois, Kansas, Kentucky, Minnesota, Missouri, Montana, New York, South Carolina, South Dakota, Tennessee, Texas, Virginia, Washington, and Wyoming. Luckily the Head, teachers and Governors stand firm. Perhaps things really are changing and transgender people will be more protected and their lives made easier. The UK government are to look at making transition much easier.

I cannot make my mind up yet about adoption. There is nothing I would like more than to be a legal member of this family but there are some things that stand in the way.

The first reason is I am still waiting for the inquest on mum. I don't want to see someone blamed for that. People can be so crafty and even though they show an open mouth after supposedly swallowing a pill, patients do secrete them or even regurgitate.

The second reason is that I wish to keep mum's name, especially now I'm in touch with her parents, my grandparents and changing my name again, would seem a slap in their faces.

The third reason is that I'm in love with Kayleigh. As an adopted daughter, our love would feel like incest. It's better that we have this small space between us even if it is largely imaginary.

Lastly if I'm adopted the council would not pay for fostering and the money Ros and Harry receive, will pay for not only my transition but also Uni. I take my time mulling this over.

At last Harry is home and we have a Sunday lunch together. My cooking skills have improved and Kayleigh and I do the whole meal, roast and sweet. We have rosé sparkling wine. When sweets are done I pluck up courage.

'Thanks all of you for inviting me firstly into your home and then for inviting me into your family.' I tell them my reasons why I don't want to be adopted. 'I just want to say, you have truly saved me. Without you, I really think I would have gone under. I had reached a point where life seemed to have no joy, no meaning, there was no future. The road of my life was completely obscured by a fog of dysphoria and loneliness. It was pointless and hopeless. Now I can see the road, it is mapped out. I need to work and work hard, but with your help, I can realise my ambitions and be a credit to myself and to you. I want to be a great lawyer, a barrister eventually. I want to be a success for myself, for you and for my mum and the Gramps. I will always wish to be a member of this loving family.

'Kayleigh, thank you for seeing something in the odd ball I was and Mum and Harry, thank you too for raising such a great daughter who could look at a loser and see the potential.'

Kayleigh holds my hand and then we clear the dishes. Harry comes into the kitchen and wraps me in his strong arms and I think he will crush the life from me.

'Never mind the paperwork, Summ. You are a member of this family and I love that you are here. Just work hard.'

'Oh I will Harry.' We kiss.

I go to mum. 'I respect your daughter and I love her. I love you too mum. I don't want to be a drain on this family, so I will stay a foster child. Maybe one day, you will want to adopt me and I will want to be adopted. I can't think of anywhere I would rather be.'

'We are glad you're here.' Harry says. 'Something you have to understand Summer and I'm not sure you do. Ros and I love each other, just we have different needs. Don't think that we will part, it's not going to happen. I spoke to Samantha about your holiday plan for us all and discussed it with Ros too. If that's the way you are going, then I think we would all like to be there for you.'

'Thanks dad.' We kiss.

'Time for bed Summ,' Kayleigh says.

The end.

Please, please leave a review. Find the page for 'The Passing of Little Tough Guy', scroll down and leave a review. You can choose any name you like. Many thanks.

Made in the USA
Middletown, DE
02 September 2017